Nonlocal Science Fiction

March 2015 – Issue #1

Daniel J. Dombrowski, editor

ISBN: 978-0-9961723-2-5

Published by:
33rd Street Digital Press, LLC
P.O. Box 9294
Erie, Pa. 16505

www.thirtythirdstreet.com
nonlocal@thirtythirdstreet.com

Table of Contents

THERE'S A SMALL CHILD IN US
WHO ONLY CARES ABOUT THE PICTURES

COVER DESIGN BY
BIOBLOSSOMCREATIVE.COM

Letter From The Editor

Dear Reader,

After months of preparation and hundreds upon hundreds of hours of hard work, the first issue of *Nonlocal Science Fiction* is complete and ready for you to enjoy. Thank you for your support in making this magazine a reality. Words cannot express how much it means to me that you backed this project and helped to bring it to life.

Despite the work that has gone into *Nonlocal Science Fiction* so far, I am reminded frequently that this is only the first step in a much larger journey. Publishing a magazine is one thing. Getting noticed and gaining a following is something else entirely. But today is not a day to worry about business and marketing. Today is a day to celebrate. *Nonlocal Science Fiction* has arrived.

Thank you, once again, to every Kickstarter backer. Thank you also to Bioblossom Creative, the wonderful design company that completed work on the fantastic cover art before I could pay for it so that I could reveal it during the campaign. And finally, thank you to the nine authors whose work appears in these pages for trusting me and taking a chance on a new venture.

I've told the story frequently of my first experience with science fiction literature. I plundered my father's book shelf when I was very young, reading *Foundation* and "A Martian Odyssey" while avoiding my school assignments. I began a journey in those early days that has led me, along a long and crooked path, to this point. Science fiction has been one of the few constants in my life. No matter where I have been or what I have been doing, I have always immersed myself in the genre.

The house where I grew up and fell in love with science fiction is located on 33rd Street, the namesake of the publishing company behind this magazine. Some day, strangers will live in that house, and I will drive by it and point it out to my kids and say, "That's where I grew up." But there will always be a part of me tucked away in the corner of my bedroom, reading science fiction on 33rd Street.

Thank You,

After you read Issue #1...

News & Announcements
Articles
Reviews
Podcasts
"Best of" Lists

...head to NonlocalSciFi.com
for sci-fi news, reviews, and more!

And be sure to follow us on social media
so you never miss a thing!

facebook.com
/NonlocalScifi

twitter.com
/NonlocalSciFi

Delivery to Venus

Written By
Robert Paul Blumenstein

For Rudolf Steiner

The ship creaked, and a rumble followed that stretched through the entire vessel until the sound culminated into a deafening crack that left the occupants wondering if the hull had been breached. A shiver ran through the entire crew of eight.

"Compensate and stabilize!" the captain shouted to his helmsman, as if she had needed to wait upon such a command.

Each shockwave passing through the ship generated from the shrinking sun had the same effect—deterioration of orbit.

They would need to deposit their cargo onto the Venusian surface soon.

With maximum cool, Agabus, the helmsman set the ship back into orbit, never doubting her ability to do so. She confirmed that the captain's order had been fulfilled and turned back to her work at the helm with a wry smile.

"He always insists on shouting. Why doesn't he use his psychopraxic skills to communicate?" she thought. "I suppose it never hurts to use the old vocal cords every once in a while, but it seems like his shouting would be awfully painful." Her dark, almond-shaped eyes twinkled as she considered what a real character Captain Fortune truly was.

The robust captain bustled about the bridge to confirm that engineering still had the engines online and that communications had sent another status report back to Earth. Satisfied, he sauntered over to the Erudition Station to consult Wandabe, the science officer.

"Captain, I believe I've located a suitable place on the surface to deliver our cargo, large enough for the shuttle to land and construct the bioshield," said Wandabe.

"Excellent. Surface temp and atmosphere?"

"The distortions in space generated by the shrinking sun are stripping the toxic gases from the atmosphere," said Wandabe. "It is aiding the cooling of the planet's temperature. Venus is rapidly morphing into early Earth-like conditions."

"But will it hold? That you can't tell me, can you?"

"No, Captain, I cannot. We do not know what will happen once Mercury is pulled into the sun. The slide has already started. I estimate that we have approximately eight hours to land on Venus's surface, construct the bioshield, and deposit our cargo safely under the shield."

"Understand this, Wandabe, the principle act after we complete our delivery is to get out of orbit so we're not pulled down onto Venus's surface. It is of prime importance that we leave no traces that we ever set foot on that planet. As second in command, you must assure me that you will make leaving orbit your foremost priority."

"Understood, Captain," said Wandabe.

The captain filled his large lungs with a reassuring breath of air, satisfied that his orders would be carried out should the landing party, which included himself, become stranded on the surface. Wandabe was from the race known as the Inviolables. It was impossible for them to make negative choices due to emotional influence. The captain was more than happy to leave the tiller in her capable hands.

"Wandabe, program the coordinates into the shuttle's guidance system. I'll let the good doctor know that he's to report to the launch bay with his bundle for the nursery. I'll need two crewmen to assist us. Assign crewman Alden, and, huh, helmsman, how would you like to be one of the first persons to set foot on Venus?"

It was hard to believe that this rocky, muddy surface would one day harbor abundant, verdurous vegetation. Agabus noted that water had already begun to form on Venus, collecting in the low spots of the planet's surface. She tested a sample of the water for density and microbial content. The water was fairly thin, similar to the newly forming air, and no microbes were detected. But it was still early.

Agabus's mind wandered. She wondered if Earth, so many millions of years before, had looked like this. The small number of earthlings left had banked all their knowledge on a theory known as solar evolution—that life will naturally spring from the proper order of conditions on a satellite or planetary body.

"Ah, Venus is taking shape nicely," she thought. Her imagination ran on a little further, and she wondered what Earth had been like not so long ago, in the early years of the 21st century. The change had taken everyone by surprise. Part of the sun's inner core had collapsed. They'd had no instruments to measure deep inside the sun's core to determine its burn and predict the disaster. The gravitational distortion had been immense, quavering the little rock known as Earth into a furious tailspin, irreparably damaging the stratopause. The little planet that was once seventy-five percent liquid water had become seventy-five percent solid ice virtually overnight, driving the remaining inhabitants underground to preserve their technology, culture, and hopefully their species.

Now, Earth was nothing more than a frigid chunk of ice orbiting the sun, preserved as nothing more than a bibliographic memory.

The ship's doctor, an elderly, white-haired man with a hundred plus years of wrinkles paving his face, watched in amusement while the young woman took her readings and made notes concerning her field observations of the planet.

"Hey, Doc, where did ya go?" asked Fortune.

Doc laughed softly. "You know, Bob, a hundred and fifty years ago, I was a lot like her—a thirsty sponge. Of course, I did all my soaking-it-up in a laboratory. It's too bad we can't leave her here along with a young, handsome stud and let them populate the place the good old-fashioned way."

"A young, handsome stud?" the captain puffed. "I hardly think either of us would be a good candidate for that role. No, she'd need someone with a little more oomph than what's left in me. But I do like your idea of doing things the old-fashioned way, especially with Agabus."

"Why, Bob, you old reprobate. You know the regulations about fraternization."

"Look, Doc, it's only in my mind."

"They tell us that's the same thing."

Fortune regarded the doctor for a moment and then grunted. After another thoughtful moment passed, he said, "You know, Doc, I hope all this cosmic memory stuff the Elder Council is banking on is actually true. It's hard to believe that man began life on Titan, moved inward to the Lost Planet and then to Mars before finally ending up on Earth. I know the dying sun should be absolute proof of the theory. I mean, here we are millions of years later, seeding a planet just like our ancestors from Mars did on Earth, but damn it, Doc, I feel lost in the eons. There's nothing to go back to on Earth, and we're supposed to slingshot ourselves around the sun, set the controls on automatic pilot, effectively kill ourselves when we enter suspended animation, and then just drift, probably forever. Ludicrous!"

"Bob, you've got a job to do. You just keep your mind on that. Besides, there's no reason to go back to Earth, except to freeze to death. At least, if we can make it out of the solar system, we might somehow find other humanoids or—"

The old doc had nothing else to say. The hope that had henceforth spewed from his mouth had become as hollow as a religious mantra. He had learned to transfer that entangled mixture of hope and despair into thoughts of some semblance of a future for mankind. A ship full of the only humans who weren't freezing to death on Earth, hibernating in deep space, propelled along with nothing more than spent fuel canisters and a vain hope that someone—or some thing—would eventually find them was about as empty as it got.

"You know what really pisses me off, Doc?"

The doctor answered with squint, crow-footed eyes, "What?"

"That we never made it out of our own solar system. That we couldn't stop fighting over this patch or that patch of frigging moon dust. That we had to hide from the general public that we had ancestors on Mars and instead, debated about what a microbe embedded in some damn Martian rock meant. The Saturn Wars. Europa. All for what? So some S.O.B. could line his damn pockets with money? To hell with the survival of our race. Just let a small cadre of pricks enrich themselves at the expense of the whole species. Damn, Doc, is that all we are?"

"No, Bob. We're hope. What in the blue blazes do you think we're standing here for? Especially ogling over some nubile, fine looking specimen of female humanity. We still have something left in these old bags of bones if we can at least appreciate a beautiful woman and dare to take her in our minds. I mean, you don't mean to tell me that's not something?"

Fortune cocked his head to one side and sized up the old geezer of a doctor and then eased out a soft chuckle. "Yeah, Doc, it's something all right. Well, looks like Crewman Alden has finished with the bioshield. Time for you to inseminate Venus. Need any help?"

"Naw, I got this one, Bob."

Captain Fortune and Agabus stood off to one side, watching the doctor place the bundle into the bioshield. The helmsman looked at her captain, wondering why she had not been ordered to return to the shuttle craft. Instead, Crewman Alden had been sent back to man the helm with specific orders to leave without them at the first sign of trouble.

"I thought you might want to watch and know what we're doing here," said Fortune.

"Oh, so he's reading my thoughts, is he?" Agabus thought.

"Yeah, I am," the captain projected into her mind.

"I suppose you're aware, then, that I know what you were thinking about standing over there with the doctor while the two of you were watching me."

"You going to turn me in?" the captain asked, this time speaking rather than thinking.

The pretty young woman giggled and then said, "Hardly; I might even be flattered to have turned my captain's head. Such naughty thoughts you have."

"Yeah, well, the end of the world kind of does things like that to a guy."

Agabus took on a purely professional tone. "Captain Fortune, why did you want me to wait here instead of manning my post?"

"Agabus, do you know what's in that bundle the doctor is leaving inside the bioshield?"

"No, sir. I've understood all along that that information is classified."

"In that bundle is the future of our species. Think of it like a loaf of bread, Helmsman. Every DNA sequence, every gene in the human species, so ordered to eventually develop into a human being. Yes, in primitive form, of course, but nevertheless, a human. A human seed, Agabus. A bun in the oven, in the vernacular of oh so long ago. Although the theory of solar evolution has been drummed into us relentlessly and more often, religiously, the Elder Council is taking no chances. They're hedging their bets, so to speak, and making sure that, as Venus evolves into a great green and blue ball, as Earth once was, that humanity will again roam the surface, just as we did on Earth, Mars, and the rest of them.

"The Elder Council feared that someone among our crew might try to mentally influence the little booger in there, shape its destiny and that sort of thing, hence all the top secret business. Hardly seems to matter now. But orders are orders..." Fortune rambled on.

"Then, why are you telling me this at this point?" asked Agabus.

"I don't know, Helmsman. Maybe I'm just sentimental. Perhaps primordial forces, locked away in my own genetic code, have emerged and have taken control of me. You know, the first man and the first woman—that sort ancient mythical stuff that our early ancestors believed. But then, here we are, observing the seed of our own species being planted on this planet, which Earth's inhabitants believed would never support life. But it is here that life will begin all over again."

"It's not really beginning all over again, Captain. It's merely being extended, given one more chance to survive and flourish."

"Good heavens, Agabus, do you think this strain will get it right this time? Or will they muck about with this wonderful gift and let it all go to hell in a handbag? We've had at least three planets, numerous moons, and billions of years to make something everlasting from our species, and we're still heading toward a dying sun. I feel like we should say some words to commemorate this occasion, but by Jove, Agabus, I'm at a loss for what to say. I swear that I am!"

Agabus took the captain's hand into hers and never once took her eyes off of the man. She saw a glisten in his eyes and knew that it was no atmospheric phenomenon. Rather, it was pain that he had carried here, to this far away world of Venus. She realized at that moment just how burdensome hope was to a person.

"This must be what they call wisdom," she thought.

"Yeah, it is," muttered the captain.

"Captain, I've just received a communiqué from the ship. Another space distortion is headed our way, and it appears to be rather large. Science Officer Wandabe believes the shockwave was caused by Mercury impacting the sun. That'll make the shockwave rather large. Wandabe recommends that—"

"Duly noted, Alden, we're on our way. Be prepared for immediate liftoff upon our arrival." The captain turned to his helmsman and asked, "You want to stay?"

"I beg your pardon?" Agabus asked, nearly bursting into laughter. "Why?"

"You know, stay here, the first man and woman. Populate the planet. Raise a garden. That sort of thing," said the captain with a boyish grin.

"I might take you up on that, Bob, but let's find another planet first."

The two turned away from the bioshield and headed back toward the shuttle craft.

"Oh, no! Wait, Captain."

"Change your mind?" the captain said, only half kidding. Then he saw the look of horror on his helmsman's face. "What's wrong?"

"My scanner; I've lost it."

"I last saw it back at the bioshield," said Fortune. Then, he remembered her setting it on the ground just before taking his hand into hers. In that moment, he had regretted being the captain. Now, he regretted not acting like one and missing the obvious.

"I'll have to go back and get it," Agabus said in a near panic.

"No, we'll go together. And stay calm. We'll make it back to the ship on time."

Once they had returned to the bioshield, sure enough, there, lying on the ground, was the helmsman's scanner, exactly where she had set the thing down. She quickly retrieved her misplaced tool and turned to leave, but she stopped dead in her tracks, her stare affixed on the bundle.

The captain hurried over to her, fearing the worst—that the bioshield had been compromised and humanity's only hope lay rotting on the Venusian soil. However, the sight that held the helmsman's and now the captain's attention was not that horrible vision at all.

From the loaf, two eyes stared out at them. No other features were visible on the mass, only the two, unblinking, staring eyes, intently focusing on the captain and the helmsman from inside the bioshield.

Neither one of them was able to move until Fortune heard the voice of Crewman Alden through his communication device, "Captain, you have less than three minutes to reach the shuttle or we're leaving without you. Your own orders, sir."

"We're on our way."

The calculations for hurling the ship into the far reaches of outer space, specifically in the direction of Orion, using the sun's gravity had worked brilliantly. The engines had been programmed to fire off the remaining fuel after passing through the Edgeworth-Kuiper Belt. The ship would hopefully not impact any of the debris in the belt. They were relying on the programming of the navigation system to accomplish that.

The entire crew would already have suspended their life functions and begun the state of hibernation by then. They would enter their pods with nothing more than a hope, or a prayer, if anyone on board still did that sort of thing, that someone—or some thing—out there would wake them up with the answer to whether or not the program had actually worked.

The captain and helmsman sat on the bridge, side by side, watching the blur of stars pass by the viewing port. They were waiting for Doc to call them to the hibernation bay. The three of them were the last members of the crew still awake. The captain and Agabus gazed into one another's eyes, reflecting serenity. Fortune had turned on the sensatron. The machine expelled wafts of extinct American tobacco smoke scent into the bridge's atmosphere and played sounds of crashing ocean water upon a long-ago shoreline. Neither Fortune nor Agabus fully understood why these sense stimulants calmed them, but they willingly accepted the innate effect on their senses. The sensatron had also softened the light on the bridge and changed the light's hue to a light orange.

The captain wondered if, upon awakening, their liberators might declare: "One Earth female, pregnant." Who knows?

Agabus then asked, "Are you sure there's not a hibernation container big enough for the two of us?"

The captain smiled. "Forbidden by order of the Elder Council."

Finally, the helmsman asked, "Bob, do we take our secret to bed with us, or should we make a log entry about what we saw inside the bioshield?"

"Well, knowing the Elder Council, they might just fetch us back to exact their absolute justice on us. I don't think we need to put that little matter into the log, do you?"

She shook her head. "But I do think that Doc ought to know."

"Why?"

"I don't know. Deathbed confession, perhaps?"

Fortune mused over her remark and then said, "Well, if you feel that way, let's tell Doc what happened when we went back. But it's not going into the ship's log, understood?"

"Aye, aye, Captain," said Agabus.

"Are you two love birds about ready to hit the hay?" the old doc asked after entering the bridge.

"I guess so," said Fortune. "I sure don't like the idea that I'm not the last to go under. You sure you'll be joining us?"

"Why wouldn't I?" Doc asked.

"Oh, come on, Doc: All that talk about being too old and just dying here on the bridge?"

"That was just talk," the doctor said. "Besides, I'd probably stay in the laboratory or my cabin." He laughed and then said, "I promise I'll put myself under."

"You'll do more than promise. I'm giving you a direct order, Doc."

"Aye, aye, Captain," the old man said. "So, any last words? Care to unburden yourselves before hitting the hay for the next three centuries?"

"I suppose I do," the captain said.

"Okay, let's have it," said Doc.

"Down on Venus, Agabus and I had to go back and retrieve a scanner that was accidentally left behind, and when we arrived at the bioshield, well..."

"Good ahead. Spit it out. What happened? You sing a lullaby to it or something?" Doc saw immediately that his little quip wasn't appreciated.

"It's okay, Doc, everything was left intact. The experiment will no doubt one day be very successful."

"Right, in a million years after the bioshield disintegrates. So what's the hoopla all about?" asked Doc.

"It's like this. After Agabus retrieved her instrument, she saw a pair of eyes on the loaf, staring at us. I saw them, too. As human as any eyes I've ever seen, just staring at us, taking us in, like it was trying to connect. Doc, do you think that's what happened? That bundle of DNA—human cellular tissue, all that stuff you guys put together—will it have some kind of memory of us?"

"The human racial memory is already in the DNA. It's going to dig up somethin' about its past. It's all there, from Saturn to Venus, billions of years of development—and un-development, unfortunately. Can't be helped. What are you worried about?"

"No, I mean conscious memory. Like its creator was there, present, at its beginning. That it'll misconstrue us as its creator and not see itself as having evolved in the natural order of things."

"I'm not so sure humans are part of the natural order of things anyway. We'll never know, really," said the doctor. "I wouldn't worry about it, Bob."

"Yeah, but I do. I can't help but feel that the thing will somehow recall the incident and see itself as *created* rather than *evolved*. That worries me, Doc. You think that's how cultures come up with creation myths?"

The old doc was tired—tired of asking questions, tired of answering questions, just plain tired of questions. Period.

"I don't know, Bob. Who does know? And anyway, you need to be getting to your pod. Maybe the answer'll come to you while you sleep." Ω

Marigold's Memory

Written By
Reva Russell English

The second time she tried to have the chip unlocated, she went into cardiac arrest, her heart's rhythm a high-pitched "eeeeeeeee" that showed itself on the monitor as a thin and serious line that stretched between the farthest cosmic reaches of an infinite point A and the farthest cosmic reaches of an infinite point B.

If there hadn't been a crash cart out in the hallway that some errant nurse had failed to put away, the defibrillator on and charging, Marigold's flat line would have been the last sound her body ever made, but, as luck would have it, when the electric shock paddles made contact with her cooling skin and sent 360 joules of electricity coursing through her heart's static muscle, she fell gently back into breath and pulse from whatever abyss the chip had beckoned her toward.

Her blood pressure found a sweet, solid footing, and her heartbeat had settled in at a respectable 74 big ones per minute, at which point the Assistant Memory Technician, Alex, said what the rest of them were thinking, "Looks to me like she can learn to live with it."

They had filed out of the room to smoke cigarettes and chortle through rattled nerves about how much higher their insurance had nearly climbed--not to mention the costs they would have incurred because of the damage to their good name. *How in God's name*--they asked each other and themselves--*had she almost died?*

Marigold dozed on inside the clinic's pristine, marble walls in an anesthetic haze, oblivious to it all.

She had tried before to get it wiped at another sonoluminescence place, one less respected and cheaper. Not that it advertised itself that way. But any business in a strip mall knows its reputation won't ever be able to really rise above its location, and Tri-County Memory Dis/Re/Unlocation Services seemed fine with the standards set before them by the cash advance place to their right and the nail salon to their left. After all, they weren't trying to reinvent the wheel or anything.

When they had failed, Marigold had assumed they were just shoddy at their work. It had seemed a reasonable explanation for why something as simple as erasing a memory chip could have been unsuccessful, and they had reimbursed her money, including the nonrefundable consult fee.

But still, it had bothered her like the catching of a slightly ragged thumbnail inside a mitten. Not one of her friends could remember ever having heard of someone's chip being difficult to unlocate. No one could even recall a story of failure from their grandparents' days back when Human Memory Management was a new field.

Memory chips weren't supposed to be *sticky* like memories were. It's why, when AnthroCyclo had developed MCNIP, or the Memory Chip and Neural Interweave Process, the world's governments had all signed on to give each citizen a chance at real happiness, a.k.a. freedom from the past. Chip implantation and unlocation held less risk than getting a cavity filled, and it was much more common—you only have so many teeth after all. Memory chips—at least by the time Marigold had been born—were standard-issue by the thousands in all newborns, each chip at least a petabyte depending on how much your parents were willing and able to subsidize the procedure.

The APGAR test, compulsory vaccination, and memory chip implantation—it was part of being born human.

Which is why Marigold had made an appointment with Avalon, and when—after they, too, had failed to clean out the chip—her Memory Consultation Coach had told her of the complications and let her watch the video after she signed yet another agreement promising never to sue, she began to truly worry that maybe it wasn't a problem of procedure at all. She began to worry about the chip.

It wasn't that the chip itself had gone bad, she knew that for certain. It did sometimes happen and was revealed in comedic, soft, stroke-like symptoms: lightly slurring speech, confusing 1's with L's, forgetting the names of people you saw every day, trying to put car keys into the wrong side of the steering column. No, chip H-342 was fine and holding onto its contents with a vise-like grip, which was what it was supposed to do—up to a point.

Marigold simply wanted someone to pry open those digital fingers and remove a few pieces of her past so she could sleep through the night. She wanted to step out into a late afternoon's light without being struck by a stab of loss like a javelin through the heart. She wanted the silverware in her top kitchen drawer to go back to just being silverware in a drawer.

The memories in that chip were not just things she wanted to forget. They were things she wanted never to have happened, things she wanted never to have known, things that, if she'd had a time machine, she would have already gone back to undo.

She wanted the memories and their Pavlovian hold on her body, emotions, and mind to cease to be, to cease to have ever been. She wanted them exiled, destroyed, annihilated.

It's why the chips existed. It's why her parents—out of their great love for her and their hope for her future—had sprung for upgrades her entire childhood.

Memory was supposed to be manageable, so that when pain, unfairness, shame or loss occurred, happiness could be restored with little more than the flip of a switch. Yet, here she was: a citizen of the richest country in the world with a head full of the highest quality memory chips money could buy, with an entire chip and its contents refusing to budge.

"What are my options?" Marigold asked the Memory Consultation Coach a week later, after Avalon had run a new battery of tests to get a better sense of why things had gone so badly. Her MCC, a bland-faced older woman named Eunice in canary-yellow scrubs, shook her head.

"Well, it's unprecedented." Eunice licked her lips. "Even when the chips were brand-new--70-80 years ago—erasure and unlocation never failed, even though sometimes the chips did. The problem of keeping memories intact and uncorrupted had to be addressed, but not erasure. If erasure has ever failed before, there's no record of it in the literature." She licked her lips again, this time holding them inside her mouth between her big, white teeth as though she needed to keep them properly corralled. When she spoke again, she lowered her eyes.

"The doctor thinks it's possible that some of the memories are..."

Eunice paused, looking for a word. "Well, that the memories from H-342 are actually..."

She coughed and cleared her throat. "That they're in your brain, not just in the chip. That somehow, they've--" She paused again, verbally helpless.

Marigold's temper flared just a bit. "That somehow they've *what*?" she asked.

Eunice squirmed and found her verb. "Leaked.*"*

Marigold's face flushed with heat. The word spread through her head like hot air filling a balloon. Seconds passed, a minute, two. Marigold waited, but Eunice had nothing more to say.

"What are my options?"

Eunice met Marigold's eyes again, briefly, and then turned to look out the window. The morning light cut across the parking lot between the branches of the gingko trees' bared limbs—a contrasting world of shadowy night and golden day. She sighed, and the fine, hairsprayed netting of her chestnut hair trembled.

"We don't know," she said, and she patted Marigold's knee with a gloved and clumsy hand.

Avalon, too, gave Marigold her money back. They didn't even charge her for the extra tests or those tests' results, which they handed her on minidrive. They wished her luck, and

Eunice and Dr. Akan walked her carefully to the door of the clinic. It was clear they didn't want her coming back. As Marigold got back into her car, big, slow, fat drops of rain started falling. She sat there—stunned and stoic—her hand on the keys but not turning them. She focused on not remembering what she now realized she might not be able to forget and counted slowly and evenly back from 100. Her hand was steady, her mind clear. She started the car and drove home.

It ended up not taking too long. For about a week, she worried at it like a loose button but from as far a distance as she could psychically manage, like she'd closed her eyes to rummage through a drawer in the dark.

One evening, when the fading, tangerine light painted the neighboring buildings in such excess that it caught her breath, she finally gave in and opened her eyes into that dark place where the chip and its contents lay waiting. She relaxed her thoughts and let them reach down the way a child's hand dips silently and hopefully into a forbidden cookie jar.

Like bones piled atop one another in the aftermath of a plague, she found them: still, stolid, unmoving. She picked up the first one she came across and held it up to herself. It was small, the size of a finger. She held it in her mind like the sacred object it was until it began to shimmer and move. Her chest tightened, and the edges of her eyes squeezed themselves closer.

It was the day he had told her of the promotion. She could smell the heat of the oven as it warmed in the kitchen. She watched again as he casually adjusted the collar of the suit jacket his mother had given him the Christmas before. His words pooled like mercury, slippery and adjustable. She let them slide and shift inside her head until everything seemed coated with them.

Then, she put the memory down and picked up the next one, the size of a jawbone, teeth still intact. It was the time he had ordered her to go lie down, like she was a child and he a weary parent who had already put up with enough for one day. She felt the years-ago pounding of her heart, the sweep of shame in her neck and face. She felt herself once again bite the insides of her mouth so as to keep herself from speaking. She watched herself and was herself as she went back and lay down between the cold and silent sheets, obedient. The tears from then mixed into the tears from now, and she cried as she had that night—again—for a very long time.

Time passed. The chip and its contents—her memories—stayed put, snug and safe somewhere in her brain. Sometimes, she felt them as an almost unbearable flood. Sometimes, they were little more than a dripping faucet--irksome when noticed but otherwise easily ignored.

Her understanding of her life took on a more serious tone, and she gradually forgot about forgetting. She laughed less but more heartily. She took naps during the late afternoon, bought new silverware, and visited her parents more often. She listened to their stories, and she told them hers. Ω

In The Days Of Still Pictures

Written By
H. C. Turk

At the desert's edge, where dry heat created transient visions, sat the town of Vargo, Dakoda Territory, population low and unknown in the year 1873. Remarkable the newcomers passing through. Miners heading for the promised platinum out west just stopping for some drugs at the saloon. Damn herd of elephants ran right through the streets once. Really tore up the place. Your big city journalist seeking the "truth of the American frontier," like a profundity misplaced. Some people stayed for one reason or none, for one duration or another. The photographer, Mizzer Benjumin Roze, had been present a month, but not many people could afford his family portraits. A traveling salesman changed that, providing Mzr. Benjumin with a plenitude of business, an enterprise to unhinge this Erth frontier.

Another recent settler initiated all this changing: Mizz Belinduh Lase, the show girl made only for looking, not a hand to be laid on her for fear of one's head being knocked across the bar. After too many weeks in the coarsest wagons on the harshest trails, with dust enough to make a crust on you, Belinduh decided she had ventured enough. After grandiose claims of new wealth spreading in the Territories like dreams in a young woman's mind, Belinduh no longer believed that Calizonia was any better than Dakoda. A job was easy to find, since she could dance. Good pay, too, with her appearance. But this wench went deeper than nipples.

Though not the first to meet the salesman, only Belinduh was driven by ambition. She needed to impress the marshal, Mzr. Frenk Jeorje. Belinduh felt that without something new about her, she would not be marrying Frenk, the latest grand desire in her life. Vargo's most respected man, Marshal Jeorje was too proper to show interest in a bar girl. He had nothing

20

against Belinduh, mind you, but Jeorje was too busy with Indyuns and elephant rustlers to be thinking of settling. He had a territory to establish, a frontier to figure. But Belinduh was sure in her heart that if the schoolmarm had her figure, Frenk would think differently. Thus, she desired from the traveling salesman something of class, a suave accessory to accentuate her feminine accouterments. Belinduh was certain that if the marshal only noticed her, he would soon discover her true worth, and then...

From her room above the saloon, bored, expectant Belinduh saw women collect about this wagon. After one look, Belinduh flung herself down the steps and ran across the street. Men stared as Belinduh lifted her hem clear of the dust. Nearing the wagon, Belinduh saw no painted slogans, no claims of "Seller To The World!" or "Finest Goods In Any Land!" The wagon was just a wooden box, but them horses seemed strange. Average looking with their black and white stripes, but they didn't move, not a flick of the ear or the first leg twitch.

"I could stand a new skillet," one lady said, "but you don't have none?"

The crowd looked to the traveling salesman standing by his wagon, contents unseen. For sure, he was some kind of foreigner, though less so than his sidekick, a dolt with a dumb smile snagged on his lips. Of this pair, the salesman was the only speaker.

"Today, ladies and gentles, we have free samples to entice you further with later goods we will be selling," he stated flatly.

From within the wagon's dark interior, the salesman's helper began handing him palm-sized boxes that meant nothing to no one.

These ladies were less than enchanted. The anxious salesman was ready to give them boxes away left and right, but only one was taken gingerly by a younger woman.

"What is it we have here?" she asked cautiously, looking down to the nearly weightless, featureless form.

"Demonstration!" the salesman cried, and displayed a box to the crowd. "With the lump on top, aim the camera toward your desired matter and press."

After the salesman casually aimed a box at the nearest woman and pressed with one thumb, a perfect photograph appeared on the cube's face, and the crowd gasped.

The ladies crowded near to see, buzzing with excitement, for the photo was not like those glass plates of Mzr. Roze. His were flat and dull in comparison, but this box displayed perfect color, perfectly clear, and seemed like a window. The convincing impression was of looking through the box to view a genuine scene, one so realistic that the observers expected the tiny woman there to move. Then all of the ladies moved, reaching up for the free boxes, the traveling salesman and his helper handing them out right and left as they had intended all along.

After a hectic moment of experimentation—a dozen rapid, beautiful pictures taken by the crowd—a wag called out from the back.

"Yeah, but can you make it rain?"

"Not for free," the salesman replied, still handing out them boxes like pails at a bucket brigade.

The crowd absorbed scores of boxes. Lots of bumps pushed, the folk learning real quick that each push produced a new image, which displaced the previous view.

"Have all the free samples wanted," the traveling salesman offered loudly. "Give them to family. Aim at everyone in your world."

It seemed he had enough for everyone in the whole Dakoda Territory. A bit of a struggle with all those reaching hands, but Mizz Lase was still one of the earliest to get hers; for upon seeing that initial image, Belinduh determined that she had found something to catch the marshal's eye. More firmly than any of those hard-working females, Belinduh pressed through the crowd to take a box, take another. Her pushing was too rough for some, however: Mizzus Dawlton, who approved of no saloon and none of their employees.

"I don't know why you would be needing any picture taking. Everybody sees all of you as it is," she admonished with a stern look toward Belinduh's decolletage.

"Yes, ma'am; thank you, ma'am," Belinduh replied, not looking to this woman, her voice as flat as a jealous hag's chest.

With two unexposed boxes secured in her arms, Belinduh made her way less forcefully through the crowd, wondering why she felt shame from a woman who found shame in other people more readily than she found skin.

Once away from the crowd, their excited sound, Belinduh felt energized, delighted at a new opportunity to entice the marshal. Frenk had been busy that day, noticing a rare brown striper outside the commonstore, figuring the rider was not the owner. How would one of those thieving Duncun brothers get such a mare? But Bil Duncun was out of the store with his bean sack and gone before the marshal could confront him. Then there showed this wagon, a crowd gathering. Frenk did not need to ask of this event, for here came Mizz Belinduh running up to tell him in person.

She seemed like a little girl with all that enthusiasm, turning them big grey eyes on him accompanied by an uncertain smile. Recalling past desires never achieved, her expression was as provisional as a fata morgana, a hot mirage suggesting scenes never realized, visual deja vu on the desert.

Frenk found himself staring at something he didn't want to see, not like this. His ultrareal image glowed from a cube. Why, he might have been trapped in there. After some bubbly words from Belinduh too quick to understand, Frenk took the second box and tried it on her. Yes, there she was in that little box, though the real Belinduh stared at her image along with the marshal. Then they had some conversation about where the boxes came from before Belinduh got down to serious business.

"At least I'll have something to remember you by," she sighed.

"Are you going somewhere, mizz?"

"No, but I guess I won't be seeing much of you in real life considering that...considering that you don't like me."

Her final words were quiet as she looked directly into Frenk's eyes, her dejection innocent and earnest.

"You know, Mizz Belinduh, I feel sorry for you."

"Why is that, Marshal, because I work in a saloon? Does that make me so unholy?"

"No, mizz, it does not. Out here, holiness ain't like in the big cities. You got to do what you got to do in the Territories, and most people will not be holding that against you. No one calls me a killer because of the Indyuns and outlaws I've had to put under. No, Mizz Belinduh, I feel sorry for you because a comely lady such as yourself could have many a man in this town permanent, but you seem to be wanting me."

"And what is wrong with you?" she snapped defensively.

Getting loud here. People on their way to join the crowd around the salesman looked over to the difficulty, but found an affair that did not concern them.

"Why, Mizz Belinduh, I'm the one most likely to be dying on you," Frenk explained, no boasting.

"Mzr. Marshal Jeorje, before our speaking here, I considered you the finest, most manly person in the Territory. Now I learn that you are yellow. To deny yourself a rightful life of family as Gahd intended is a cowardly thing and one I'm ashamed of in my marshal and my...." But Belinduh had no final term, had no ultimate place in Frenk's life.

Not too many people could call the marshal yellow and continue with normal living. No flinching in Belinduh, however, as she flung out her final judgment and harshly walked away.

She left the box with her image. The one she took emulated her heart, which held a hyperreal version of the marshal, an image lacking the verisimilitude of requited love.

The boxes were everywhere in Vargo, all the people having fun, except the photographer, who was out of business. Belinduh placed her picture cube on the dresser in her room above the saloon where she worked that evening without thoughts of the marshal—which was unusual—until he arrived, which was rare.

Ensconced in an ambient haze of liquor fumes and smoke, Belinduh was working, not worrying. Then she saw him. The miners and pachypokes didn't notice, standard customers listening to Belinduh sing with the piano man, her voice genuinely bad. Her superior art came in the form of kinesis. Belinduh began dancing. Her kicks showed petticoat, and the room roared.

The marshal didn't notice. Glancing at the bar, Belinduh saw that Frenk had been joined by a cavalryman, unmistakable in his dark blue culottes. Kaptain Feelds scouted the Territory and reported to the marshal. Belinduh thought of a planned rendezvous and was saddened, feeling that nothing had changed with her and Frenk, nothing improved.

"The Suex got a herd of mustangs I have never seen before," Feelds described. "They say they're so fast you can't catch them or shoot the rider."

"That ain't true."

"The Indyuns think it's true, so they think they can get away with about anything. What else they say is real, Frenk. Those mustangs aren't striped like a regular horse, but the same color all over. Pink, pink as a wet dream."

The Suex had never settled well after losing their territory to the colorless settlers. The fundamentalists of the tribe had promised retribution. Led by an old but still active warrior named Dogfeather, several dozen Suex had split from their people. They called themselves the True Suns of the Spirut and were attacking settlements ever nearer Vargo. No one killed yet, just some razzing. The settlers had a lot of guns, few for the Indyuns. So far, this was the major peace keeper. Frenk knew Dogfeather from a stint in the cavalry years ago. The two were not friends but could talk.

"Maybe I can learn what the Dog is thinking," Frenk offered.

"He ain't getting no milder with age."

Due to the crowd's loud sound, the two men quit talking and turned to the stage, seeing that Belinduh was getting no milder herself. Come to tell, her skirts were flying higher than the marshal had ever seen. All that kicking was about to show body from the bottom. Though Belinduh still smiled, her demeanor had an ornery taint. The crowd was nighing a riot, so it seemed, with all their shouting and frothing. Hunched over his keys, the piano man punched out a fury near to match Belinduh's display. But no one considered his sound a glory.

Frenk and Kapt. Feelds stared at this wondrous seam, sinuous up the back of Belinduh's leg, a line alive with implication. Then they watched a riot begin, for one burly gent with a smile more ornery than Belinduh's joined her onstage, at first doing some stomping to delight the crowd. Then he tried to delight himself, hands all over the show girl, who stopped dancing, yanking them big hands away. The piano player understood something was wrong just as the marshal leapt upon the stage, nothing frantic about him.

The piano man was all bent around on his stool trying to see this while his fingers still flipped keys. See Belinduh try to smack the guy away, get his lips off her nose, get that hot breath off her eyeball. She was doing little good. The marshal did much better, grabbing the heavier man by his beard and yanking. That action yanked the sound clear out of the saloon. The big man, his eyes watering, stared at Frenk as Belinduh stepped away. Everyone heard the marshal's words.

"You will cease, or I will make your life a little harsher."

That made the crowd loud again, though they heard the burly man call Jeorje a cat bitch's brother. They saw the stage invader reach out to shove the marshal's head down around his hips. Frenk was more decisive, being professional. So out he comes with his rocket gun to meet the gent's cheek with a fluted cylinder.

Slow and certain, Frenk stepped off the stage, not needing to look behind to know that the bearded grabber required his best effort just to get off on his own accord, his own feet. Frenk returned to the bar, finishing his wetdrug beside Feelds.

Being an artist, Belinduh continued despite social adversities. As the piano man returned to his tune, Belinduh began dancing again, her enticing smile causing the crowd to swoon. She ended her act by turning, bending, backside out, skirts up in a flash, most of this flesh covered, but shapes and associations to be fondly recalled through many a long day of hard working. Like a time traveler, Belinduh created a hot mirage of desire for the future.

The marshal would not forget this himself, Belinduh soon off to incomparable applause, replaced by a pair of dancers equally energetic but not so fine, not so fabulous.

Belinduh slept well that evening, not bothered by her ordeal. She was moved by the marshal, however. Though she determined he had been doing his job onstage, in her heart she felt that he was protecting not his town but his gal.

Just a glimpse at that wonderful image before sleeping, so deep in the box it seemed Frenk looking out from a home they could share. Next morning, Belinduh studied it careful, for the picture had changed. No color now, the marshal all grey. And the image seemed flatter. Belinduh felt a terrible loss, thinking of the marshal so emotionally near last night, farther away now, the same as his image. But Belinduh had a solution, if not for Frenk, then for his facsimile. Why, if a photograph goes bad, take it to the photographer to fix it.

In a rush, Belinduh was on her way to the hotel with her box. No use looking for the salesman, who had left the day before. After flying up the stairs, she stormed through the door to confront the busy man with her problem. Mzr. Roze, however, did not show the appropriate concern, heated by the wrong vision.

"Mizz Belinduh, you were truly wondrous last evening."

"Mzr. Roze, I'll ask you to concentrate on my business, not your pleasure. I have lost the picture in my box."

She was confident that he would find a solution, for darkroom gear lay all about him; and scattered everywhere were the salesman's cubes: some blank, some colored, some fading.

Roze did not care to retrieve lost images. He was trying to figure the camera, not the sensitized emulsion. Since yesterday, he had been trying to open the cubes, but no luck. Not beating nor prying nor coaxing would part its pieces. The town blacksmith with red heat and hammer could not dent the near weightless box, the local locksmith finding no way inside. Roze wanted to remove the plate, to figure the lens, but had learned nothing.

"You had better be learning something," Belinduh insisted, "if you want me as a customer. How about mending them instead of trying to bust them open?"

"I figure that to be a waste of time."

"Don't you dip your pictures to make them appear?" Belinduh wondered, waving at the smelly chemicals.

"Yes, but first you have to remove the plate from the camera."

"Perhaps they're all of a piece in these new cameras."

"My chemicals are expensive, mizz."

"I know how to pay. I've been paying since I arrived."

To keep Belinduh around a little longer and to lessen her anxiety, he would try. A common gold toner, perhaps, to make the image permanent, impervious to the vagaries of chemical decay.

That didn't work, for after a healthy dip in a prepared solution, Belinduh's box came out backwards. Roze explained the term "negative," but Belinduh didn't care. She wanted her marshal back.

Further ad hoc experiments produced no positive results. Disappointed, Belinduh left with her box, hoping that the image might return after a spell. Worse events had befallen her, so Belinduh would not be pining, especially considering the affection Frenk had shown her in clubbing that man onstage. Bolstered by the potential of this feeling, Belinduh proceeded to her room in improved humor, a condition that ended after meeting this elephant.

No longer fearing the loss of Frenk's image, she decided to push the bump and try her changed camera. This towing elephant was tied nearby, so Belinduh aimed the camera and thumbed. Quicker than spit shot out a black streak that looked like a beam of light through a knothole except, well, negative. Appearing on the elephant was an image equal in size to the box's picture, but positive, a grey portrait of Jeorje on the dead animal's flank.

The dead animal. The beam touched hide, left its perfectly clear mark, and the elephant dropped without a sound or twitch. The plainest collapse you could imagine, and there the creature lay, dead. The picture remained.

Belinduh dropped her box and stumbled away, unable to believe she had killed so quickly, so queerly. Belinduh would recover. The elephant's owner was not so malleable, outside minutes later to find his dead animal and witnesses. The story sure sounded stupid to him, but he was rendered stupid by the loss. So he snatched the dropped box and stomped off to have the murdering wench arrested.

The marshal did not take kindly to crazy people and was about to situate this man inside a jail cell. First he strode outside to prove how crazy the elephant owner truly was. Jeorje then proceeded to instantly kill Pastor Smellin's horse. And their world was changed forever.

Days later, things had settled enough for the marshal to be on with his business of Indyuns. Several horses and two people lay dead because of the countless boxes the photographer had modified for an impressive fee. But these practical townsfolk learned soon enough to watch their boxes better than their loaded guns, and the effortless killing ended. Frenk was going to arrest Roze or the salesman for causing this trouble, but there was no law against making guns or selling them, only against arming Indyuns and murdering folk or their livestock. The marshal thought of arresting all the killers in town, but he was one. Belinduh, too, but Frenk was keeping away from her, having gotten carried away on her behalf and knowing why. Emotion is an indefensible weapon.

Funny thing about them boxes. The ones not done over by the photographer dissolved after turning grey, leaving a little dust pile, nothing more. Many a man now carried a toned box at his side, but none for the marshal. Not the equipment he was issued. The only box Frenk had was in his desk, of this dancer. Dust now. For work, he stuck with his rocket gun, something he could understand: pointed metal casings with holes in the back and powder inside. Smack the back with the gun's hammer and the rocket went shooting out the barrel. Simple enough, but how did that black light work? Like hell, Frenk thought. Like something from Saten.

Frenk rode out of town, headed for the True Suns' encampment. He thought of visiting the Duncuns, whose spread was sort of on the way, thought of killing two birds with one bone. But how many problems can you handle in one portion of a lifetime? He relished the ride to Dogfeather's encampment, if not the confrontation. Up the next morning after a long day's ride, first thing he did was sling a foxtail on his shoulder, the Suex sign for peace. Otherwise Frenk would be like a porcupine with all them spears in his ribs as soon as he neared the True Suns' camp.

They saw him all right, and weren't hiding, Indyuns in the brush making more noise than a colorless man. Frenk soon arrived at the camp. No mistaking the Suex, not with their bright blond, frizzy hair and nearly black skin. They walked or worked or rode their stripers, but not a one would look at Frenk. They couldn't kill Jeorje because he was known—the colorless marshal—and had the foxtail. They couldn't kill him, so they looked clear through.

Minutes later past this thicket, Frenk got a glimpse of roped horses, not like those around him, but solids colored pink. Pink as an elephant's tongue. On he went, arriving at a Suex willing to look at him. Dogfeather stood by a tent, ankles crossed like a big town dandy. With his long hair and headband, the Dog was all Indyun, but he reached to shake Jeorje's hand as he dismounted just like a colorless person. Though the marshal expected some conversation, wordless Dogfeather lifted the tent flap to deliver a horrible shock, no more sound from him than one of them boxes.

Scores and scores of the salesman's boxes filled the tent, each with a negative image. Each deadly. Dogfeather dropped the flap and looked to Frenk with a gesture, his thumbnail raked straight before his eyes: Suex for finality. The end.

No peace sign made would protect him at the Duncun spread, so Frenk approached like an Indyun: on foot espying, low in the brush. A lot of horses corralled there, Jeorje figuring that the Duncuns would have a bill of sale for not a one. A couple dead bodies lay about, but these deaths were free, a gift from the Indyuns.

Just east of their cabin, the two older Duncun brothers lay near their horses, no spears or holes in their clothing. Pulling away one man's shirt, Jeorje found multiple pictures on his torso, voluptuous brands of dead imagery. Perfect pictures of a brilliant cloud, the end of Vargo, some emu. Frenk wondered how much tin the photographer had received from the Indyuns for selling them all those boxes. Jeorje guessed these Duncuns may have been thinking serious about getting themselves a pink mustang or two. Frenk knew that Roze would not be in Vargo when he returned. But, by Gahd in Heven, the marshal would have him hanged one day. All this thinking as he glanced inside the cabin—no one there to kill him—then returned to the second brother, Jeorje hoping to find a rocket wound, something real, something reasonable. He discovered a genuine fiction impossibly foreign.

The clearest, sharpest image on the man's belly of a, a monster. Something with arms and legs, but too skinny, obtrusive knobs for joints, skin textured like bark, bulging eyes high in a terrible head, a round mouth like a navel—the evilest fiend from any man's blackest nightmare, here delineated perfectly, as clear as death.

Where in the world had that picture been taken? Frenk wondered as he stumbled into the cabin, a part of him still professional, but most of the man shaken as deep as dreams. He stepped through the back door to find the next fiend.

Outside in the dirt lay the Duncuns' granddad. Though all dead, only half of him was normal. The man's upper body was as thin as tanned hide, his skull and torso squashed flat as though run through Saten's clothes wringer. But no blood, no guts squeezed out, just a body thin as skin to the hip, of normal thickness below. The nearby soil held a group of odd dents like the tracks of a mechanical animal. Jeorje knew nothing of this, but would not forget. He sure would not forget that body. The marshal had seen men with the damnedest holes in their heads and faces, but only this made him sick.

No puking, but stumbling through the cabin like a drugnk, on his horse in time to hear Bil Duncun and his father come to kill him, for who had destroyed their family but this lawman?

Jeorje smacked his nag and ran for Chary Chasm. Behind came hollering followed by wild shots, real rocket arms, not them heathen beams. The marshal stayed low, face in the mane, on the trail to the rope bridge, his brilliant mare not hesitating on the log surface. Frenk was halfway across when the Duncuns reached the chasm to commence careful firing. But Frenk's horse did not panic, over without a wound.

Knife in hand, Frenk leaped off, pretending to hack at the supporting ropes as rockets flied past. Too much cover for the Duncuns to see how shaky he was making the bridge. They would have to walk over real careful. Of course, they didn't follow on horseback just to fall a hundred feet dead. Of course, the marshal didn't ruin the bridge, for he might be running again someday.

On his horse, a moderate pace back to town, Frenk in need of some drugs, hoping Belinduh would be in her room, not near the bar, the marshal having faced enough terror for one portion of his lifetime.

Bad shape, their prospects, in the following days. His scouts eying the Indyuns like lovers, Kaptain Feelds had formulated a plan. The townsfolk had their share of black beams, but Dogfeather considered his new weapons a direct sign from Gahd for His True Suns to regain their land. Any day now. So Feelds was sending an entire regiment. A nervous town, this. Not much entertainment, either, since Belinduh had abandoned dancing for sweeping the saloon, her remuneration three squares a day. But no bed, for she had moved, mostly staying awake in a room across from the marshal's office; for if he would not arm himself with those best, black weapons, his lover would. Another person parked nearby had a different relation, a young man with a diminished family biding his time for revenge.

The killers came one morning. Not Suex, but the traveling salesman crying out to a developing crowd that he would buy back every box, his partner holding out handfuls of coins, but no takers. The damn stuff was foreign, and made of silver. The crowd liked to kill them both, but settled for terrible oaths against their livestock. Sell the weapons they needed for worthless coins?

"What locus is this where silver grows like stone?" the salesman shouted. "And 'gold'? An element unknown to our industries!"

Bad bartering here. Too late in the marshal's eyes for restitution regardless. Jeorje parted the crowd like a steamer on the seas and jerked the little salesman clean off his seat, pointing for the sidekick to join them or catch a rocket with his eyebrows. After a cluck from the salesman, the dumb-faced partner complied.

Jeorje told some store owner to get that wagon over to his office. Clambering up to the seat, the man slapped the reigns, and—what?—there he was on the wagon before the jail, no trail left behind, still not a move from the horses. Well, the man understood right away, heading for the saloon to hit them drugs, thank Gahd for chemistry.

Looking up, Jeorje saw the wagon ahead of him instantly, impossibly, and got angry. He locked both foreigners in a cell, then left before finding the need to club them senseless.

Aided by neighbors, Frenk tried to enter the wagon. He found no door, and beating on this "wood" meant nothing, for the big box was built just like the little ones. The most aid the townsfolk rendered was to stop Frenk when he pulled his gun and swore to blow them foreigners back to whatever hell they came from.

"Marshal, you're a man to be waiting for the judge, aren't you still?" the barber pleaded, and damned if Frenk didn't have to agree.

Though relegating violence to future jurisprudence, Jeorje went inside to give that salesman a piece of his mind he couldn't stand no more. But the salesman and his partner were gone. The cell door was still locked, bars on the window intact, no hole in the wall. The elephant thieves in the adjacent cell had heard nothing, and couldn't see through the damn wall, marshal. Jeorje ran out the back door to find the salesman destroying an Indyun.

With only a knife and sand-colored clothing, this was a Suex scout, the kind sent in pairs before a major attack. Frenk hoped the second hadn't seen his brother die, else all the Suns would be on the town at once. This one would do no reporting, because he was being wrung like clothes through a machine made of nothing the marshal could discern, the integral stand leaving marks in the dirt Jeorje had first seen at the Duncuns'. The traveling salesman was pushing the Indyun through, an unnerving groan sounding as the Suex exited fabric thin. Though apparently a lifeless device, the machine was clothed, dressed exactly like the salesman's partner.

Upon seeing the marshal, the salesman swayed a quick move near the machine, which plumped up into the partner, standing up straight, same dumb smile, the semi-processed Indyun falling to the dirt, half in a thud, half in a fabric slap.

Curiosity was no weakness with the marshal, so he pulled his gun to kill them both without wondering further what was transpiring. But the salesman told him, and Frenk listened.

"We are looking for someones," he began. "We have to find them before they become weighty. We would use the cameras, which image the truth through any disguise. But you modified the notifiers in a manner impossible to predict. We cannot machine your people to find them," he stated, making an odd, jerking gesture to the Indyun. "This gear would change the escapers back against their wills, but any organism of yours it...ends."

No more talking from him, he and his "partner" moving off, though not exactly walking. Jeorje was not going to tell them to halt or get back in the cell. Out with his gun, aim right at the head, the fire and smoke doing nothing but frightening the townsfolk out front, the rocket smashing against the salesman's skull, a couple more shots for him and his sidekick, but they did not seem to notice, did not seem to die.

Then they were gone. The marshal just stood there. Felt remarkably calm considering. Then all the citizens came running back to say that the foreigners had entered their wagon and left.

"Got away," Frenk explained. "They got away."

Ignoring the queries and cries from behind, he entered his office to be alone.

That didn't last. Before the marshal could clean his gun or steady his thinking, through the walls came a whooping to raise his hair, for the True Suns of the Spirut were charging along the streets of Vargo.

Gahd alive, those mustangs were fast. Though the Indyuns hollered a holy racket, their weapons were silent. Black beams speared through the streets, the colorless folk's horses dropping calmly, but no persons, for they were deep within their buildings. But the townsfolk also had weapon cubes. After three Suex hit the dust, a beam shot out to strike a pink horse. Perhaps that romantic rumor was based on truth, for the mustang did not die. But damned if it remained a horse.

The mustang changed and shrunk, dumping its rider, turning into that heinous creature seen by Jeorje as a picture on dead skin. Without further beaming, all the mustangs threw the Indyuns, returning to their true form. And the street was filled with horrified Suex and fiend creatures that scurried away with a graceful stride contrasting with their hellish countenance.

A foreign rain began falling, for there came the traveling salesman leaning by his partner, who was a different device this time, one filling the air with a fog of droplets that moved sideways quicker than those fiends. And there was a town full of Indyuns and colorless folk trying to blast each other with cameras.

Plenty of dead horses, but most people still stood. Then the salesman's sidekick-device sucked the rainfog back in and returned to standing and smiling. Having gotten off not the first shot, Frenk walked outside cautiously, trying to avoid being trampled by all those Suex running like crazy, having had enough evil for that portion of their lifetime. They didn't bother with no erthly guns.

Bil did. Bil Duncun had seen everything and was moved, but not enough. Despite startling scenes beyond any human's experience, Duncun remained human, retaining his vengeance, stepping out to shoot Frenk directly in his spine, the marshal dead without suffering.

Irrespective of recent screams and the subtle terror of scurrying creatures' feet, the most horrifying sound was the former dancer across the street shrieking from her heart as she aimed a box at retreating Duncun and squeezed and squeezed and....

He was off like any decent person in a minor hurry, most of the Suex fled, a lot of people collecting around the marshal, the dead marshal.

Belinduh ran to him. The stricken lady would of course fall to the man loved, never her lover, but she did not touch him. Damaged emotion destroying her visage, Belinduh stumbled to Frenk, bending quickly to rip his gun from its holster, turning at once to run hard toward the salesman, weapon cocked.

Just as this huge ball of creatures arrived around the corner. The heinous fiends had come and gone so quickly that the townsfolk tried to imagine them side effects of spoilt drugs. But even with the Suex and black beams and vanishing horses to occupy their senses, every person seeing the beasts knew them real. Here they were returned in a bunch, all the freaks packed tight like a handful of popcorn, but this ball twenty feet in diameter, the creatures pointed every which way. A few paces removed, Belinduh looked up to see them real, experiencing them more clearly than a mere nightmare. She smelled their pungent oils, saw that textured skin, the shape of their limbs, all true as any living thing she knew. And she could see expression in those glistening eyes, see mouths quiver, chests pumping air. At the bottom, the ball was supported by funny feet that only the marshal had seen before, the salesman's partner returning to the wagon with this creature collection stuck to him.

He commenced to stuff them into the wagon's rear. Ahead, the traveling salesman for the first time seemed pleased as his partner became that dumb smiler once more.

Turning to the nearest person, the salesman commented to Belinduh, "They cannot hide when they're themselves."

Seeing Belinduh's face, he understood fear. He could not bear to hear her shriek again.

"You did this," Belinduh confronted him with a loud, breaking voice. "You changed all these things, so I think you can change the marshal back. And I think you better, or I had better kill you."

The salesman agreed, not fearing the gun, but the fact.

"Dying is failure," he told her. "Making dying makes us wrong. Then to change this is yes, but not without changing too much." And he seemed sad, seemed a failure.

"If it is wrong, you had better fix it," Belinduh cried, "if you are any sort of decent person!"

She aimed the gun at the salesman and his partner, such a hole in her heart that she could kill them both without thinking. Belinduh's rockets wouldn't do it, perhaps her ethic. Foreign or familiar, the weary salesman moved away. Then he stood before the marshal, buildings away in a step, Belinduh having to whirl and run down the street to gain him.

"Too much, too much I would have to change to fix the dying. And no saying what manner would result. Too much I've forced by now. Supposed I'm asking, not making. Should I make a new mode as last repair?"

Belinduh pushed her way through the crowd, but would not look down to Frenk. The salesman and sidekick beside the body were given plenty of room.

"Well, if you can fix him, you had better, because you know it is right!" she cried, face uncontrollable, weakened by her damaged passion.

Convinced by her ardor's hot mirage, the salesman saw the need for a timely change. Right before every man jock of them, he swayed near his partner, which melted and swelled until there stood an object the townsfolk would have to walk around for minutes just to get a good look situated in their heads.

"A while appliance, to put him back when he was before," the salesman told Belinduh. "But not even a [ ] can tell what other will not be as previous. With this, the world as it is can't stay."

"I don't want this world," Belinduh whispered, Belinduh wept.

Though not readily evident, the "while appliance" had a body-sized aperture through which the salesman inserted the marshal. Jeorje was then completely within an object smaller than himself. As nothing transpired immediately, the salesman traveled away with one step, returning with a half-flat Indyun and a similar Duncun, whose visages made the townsfolk want to pray real serious or vomit with similar intensity.

Belinduh just wanted her love returned, her life's emotion manifested as the marshal.

Perhaps the salesman sensed her depths upon saying, "These are the important," for the salesman had ended this pair himself.

But an instant. In went the True Sun and Duncun, and there stood Frank George just stepping from his office, feeling a mite odd, and with a memory not what it used to be. From out back came this Sioux Indian with his straight black hair, looking good and confused but continuing with his business, probably a job at the saloon sweeping up behind paleface barflies after they had drunk their fill of whiskey. That's where the senior Duncan was headed, needing either more booze or more God in his life.

31

Belinda felt so strange. She looked to the traveling salesman and his dumb sidekick, who were trying to sell rainmakers to the townsfolk. Being sensible people, they laughed the two out of town. Then all these horses approached—bay and black and roan—their riders with tight, blue breeches and percussion sidearms scattering stray hogs and children. No one could figure why a whole regiment of cavalry had come to a place as peaceful as Fargo, Dakota Territory.

"On maneuvers," Captain Fields explained.

Still uncertain in her...emoting, Belinda finally saw something clear, something completely welcome. Marshal Frank was walking toward her, a man she adored who had no interest in a bar girl, a common dancer known to show her knees. He had found a vision in his desk: a tintype of Miss Lace given him as a memento when she was especially depressed. This was something good to look at, a formal portrait of Belinda all poised like a lady. But the marshal felt the need to examine the real person instead of her image; for one was kinetic and completely alive, the other just a still picture.

The salesman's wagon rolled slowly from town, the people who had gathered going about their affairs. And the marshal proceeded, approaching the lady.

"I was wondering if you might have a sarsaparilla with me, seeing as how neither of us appears to be, uh, occupied," he invited.

No more talking need be done, Belinda replying with a smile, taking the marshal's arm, feeling fantastic, feeling him not merely beside her but completely within, apprehended by her heart. And she walked with the man she wished for her beau, not concerned with vagrant memory, grateful alone for recent gain. Regardless of potential, of further dreams to be fulfilled, Belinda in that moment longed for stasis in her life, convinced that her emotions had progressed enough; for what could surpass the epitome of feeling that Frank had secured with his touch? And here was her wish, to hold this sensation, stopped in stride forever, her emotion the mark of a justified life, not like a tomb, but a photograph. Ω

Mazep-fal

Written By
Daniel J. Dombrowski

For Sarah

By the evening of the second day, Ephed understood in earnest why most of his tribe-mates made this journey when they turned sixty. He had heard them speak of the challenges of the *Mazep-fal*, but he'd always assumed that they were exaggerating. After walking the path, few could recall more than brief flashes of what had happened.

At ninety-six, Ephed was the oldest Bellatani to undertake the pilgrimage in nearly ten thousand years. He would have made the journey at sixty, but the Council had denied his petitions for the better part of four decades. Each rejection had stung. He was the *Trachol-ra*, the young one, though that honorific had fallen into disuse over the past few decades for obvious reasons, and he deserved respect.

No one knew what would happen when he set foot on the hallowed ground at Endur's Temple, and that scared many of the Belletani. The Council had stoked that fear, and their continued marginalization of Ephed had made him an artifact, a curiosity to be debated or avoided rather than an honored and hopeful symbol for the future. His aching body was not alone in pining for the days of his youth.

Youth was, of course, a relative term for the Belletani of Albea. The Council members, despite the airs they assumed, were mentally and physically young, just like everyone else. But every Bellatani was, by some measure, roughly 30,000 years old—except for Ephed.

Azon, a wise, old Beauceron who was serving as Ephed's guide for the *Mazep-fal*, rose to his feet, turned in a circle, and then lay down again next to the meager fire. The dog had been a patient companion, leading Ephed along the ancient path that only he and his brothers could navigate.

Ephed had kept his mind occupied throughout the journey by committing a series of landmarks to memory—two trees that had grown around and trapped a boulder, managing to lift it several feet into the air, a dry creek bed littered with pearlescent shells picked clean by scavengers, a narrow canyon that had threatened to close overhead and block out the sun at times.

It was a habit left over from a childhood spent exploring the forests near his home. But he knew he wouldn't remember any of it after completing the *Mazep-fal*. He would be relying on Azon to lead him back after the rebirth.

The journey home would be faster. Most emerged from the *Mazep-fal* about forty years younger on spry legs. There had been some debate about whether Ephed would follow that same pattern and begin a new life in his fifties or if he would return to his twenties. The gods had been silent on the matter.

The gods, in fact, had been silent for most of Ephed's life. His conception had been an immense and celebrated surprise. His birth had been the first in the recorded history of the Belletani. He had been more than a curiosity in his early years. He had been a celebrity, the savior incarnate.

The population of the Belletani had remained constant for millennia. The old and the sick had always found new life in the *Mazep-fal*, a gift bestowed by the god Endur, the creator, after his brother Etnu had stolen the Belletani's ability to reproduce.

The Mystics had long predicted the coming of the *Trachol-ra*, the birth that would signal the beginning of a new era of prosperity for the Belletani, but Ephed's birth had changed nothing. No other children had been conceived, though not for lack of trying, and the Mystics had slowly fallen out of favor.

To their credit, the holy men had continued to support Ephed for as long as possible, perhaps realizing that their only hope of ever regaining their former position in society rested on his proving to be the savior of the Belletani after all.

The Mystics had been replaced unceremoniously as the primary rulers of the Bellatani by the Council, a group of bureaucratic leaders whose positions had been granted so long before that no one could remember the mechanism. Nor had anyone challenged their right to rule when the Council sought to depose the Mystics. The Bellatani chose to respect the decisions they had made in past lives, even if the reasons were no longer apparent.

The Council had assumed the responsibility of granting access to the *Mazep-fal*, and they had been unanimous in their decision to bar Ephed from the path, a strategic move that had further marginalized the Mystics and their false savior.

All of this had taken place more than a lifetime before, and Ephed was the only member of the Belletani who still remembered it first-hand. But that would all change soon. He was on the path, and the path was all the mattered.

Ephed laid back and looked at the stars, picking out familiar constellations. Azon rose and settled next to his charge, sharing his warmth now that the fire had turned to embers.

Ephed drifted off to a dreamless sleep, uncertain what to expect in the coming days.

On the morning of the third day, it began to hail. Ephed and Azon took shelter in a nearby outcrop of rock. The thin, bleached-white clothing that all Bellatani wore while completing the *Mazep-fal* offered little protection from the elements.

Azon paced impatiently at the entrance to the small cave, snapping occasionally at a stray piece of hail, more upset about the delay than Ephed, who sat and rested his chin on his hands. He was also impatient, but at the same time, he was grateful for the additional rest period after two days of ten-hour hikes. He would make up time later and complete the journey in the prescribed six days. He pulled a dry biscuit from the bag he wore over his shoulder and chewed it slowly.

As the sun rose in the sky behind the thick layer of storm clouds, the hail turned to a heavy rain, and the beating of the large drops on the rocks over Ephed's head reminded him of the drums at his *Mazel'nact,* the celebration the night before a tribe-mate left for the *Mazep-fal*, a night usually filled with merriment when the newest pilgrim said goodbye to his or her old life.

But Ephed's first *Mazel'nact* had been subdued. Nearly half of the tribe had remained at home, silently protesting the Council's decision to allow Ephed to walk the path. They had been heeding the words of the Mystics, some of whom had gotten wind of the Council's impending decision and had come out of seclusion to denounce Ephed as a false prophet, an agent of Etnu sent to pollute the *Mazep-fal* and rob the Bellatani of the life-giving gift of Endur.

They had proclaimed to all who would listen that allowing Ephed to walk the path would reignite the war between Endur and Etnu and that the Bellatani would all suffer as a result. They had spoken of plagues, pestilence, and the like—all of the things that holy men usually warned of which never actually arrived.

Ephed had never claimed to be a prophet—true, false, or otherwise—and he disliked being told that he wanted anything other than what every member of the tribe took for granted: the safety and security of life that the *Mazep-fal* represented.

The rain stopped in the early afternoon. Ephed and Azon emerged from the rocks, determined to use the latter half of the day to make solid progress. The ground, now soft and spongy after soaking up the heavy shower, pulled at the sandals on Ephed's feet with every step. The sharp slap as they broke free from the mud and struck the bottoms of Ephed's feet provided the cadence for his hastened march.

The sun emerged from behind the rapidly fleeing clouds and beat down on the marshy landscape, and a fine mist, which seemed to rapidly solidify into a cloud at ground level, rose in every direction. Ephed walked blindly forward for several more hours, trusting Azon to guide him along the path.

They continued on until well after the sun had set over the hills to the east, and that night, both travelers fell asleep while their fire still burned brightly.

They awoke to clear skies and a bright sun on the fourth day. Pockets of fog still filled the depressions in the landscape and created the illusion of a flat plain spread out before them.

Ephed, having spied the lowlands in the distance the day before, had looked forward to an easy day's walk on mainly even terrain, but Azon turned sharply north as they approached the base of the hills they had been crossing and followed the uneven path where the slopes met the plain.

The pair pressed on as the sun climbed higher and burned off the fog. Ephed looked longingly at the flats to his left, a mottled carpet of bright greens and dark, rick browns. His feet were calloused and hard from a lifetime of labor, but the rocky ground of the path was unforgiving. His thin sandals offered little protection.

At mid-day, they approached a rock fall. Ephed had seen the obstruction from a distance, and he had hoped that Azon would veer before they reached it. The dog approached the pile of rocks, sniffed them, and then sat, looking back at Ephed with his head cocked to the left.

It was considered blasphemy to allow obstructions to remain on the path.

Ephed walked around the rocks and continued along the base of the hills, hoping to bypass the chore, but Azon didn't budge. He'd been trained by the Mystics, who walked this path regularly when no pilgrims were making the journey, and he knew what was required.

The rocks were a mix of sizes, ranging from gravel to small boulders that Ephed knew he would have had a hard time lifting even in his younger days. He sighed and began gathering some of the smaller rocks, filling his arms and then dropping each load several feet away from the path.

Azon wagged his tail and barked happily.

The sun rose higher in the sky and beat down on Ephed's bare scalp. He wetted a cloth in a rapidly evaporating pool of rainwater and sat down as the sun approached its zenith, exhausted and unsure of how he would move the final few rocks, all of which weighed at least as much as he did and some of which had embedded into the soft soil where they had landed at the bottom of the slope.

His searched his memories, trying to remember a technique or a trick he might have used to clear large stones from his parents' fields before a first planting. But it had been so long ago, and most of the memories of his youth were hazy at best.

There was one memory—one person—who did stand out from his younger days, someone he could still see vividly with no effort. It helped that he had seen her again about twenty years later when she had returned from her *Mazep-fal.*

Marni had been his first. The fact that she had been assigned to him had made little difference to either of them. There had been an instant connection, and they had fallen deeply in love and spent three wonderful years together. Ephed could still see the sparkle in her green eyes, the way the sun shone through her auburn hair as she ran ahead to one of their hiding spots.

He could also see her standing before the Mystics, trying desperately to come up with some explanation as to why she was not yet pregnant. She was the assigned companion of the *Trachel-ra,* chosen by the gods to be the mother of a new generation of Belletani. Even though no one else had successfully conceived a child after Ephed, it was still believed that his seed would be their salvation.

But the couple had had no success, though their passion for each other had never ceased. Marni had been deemed unworthy by the gods. The Mystics had torn the couple apart and assigned a new companion to Ephed over his objections.

It made no difference that he and Marni would have been split up eventually no matter the outcome of their coupling, a fact that Ephed had learned much later. The next generation of Belletani could not have sprung from a single couple. Ephed was to be tasked with impregnating every woman in the tribe that the gods deemed worthy.

He had been assigned another companion immediately, and while his young body had been willing, his mind had resisted, at least for a time. Eventually, he had given in to the advances of his new companion, a particularly beautiful young woman who was apparently the second favorite of the gods.

He'd had many companions over the next thirty years, none of them any more successful than Marni had been. Marni, for her part, had born the pain of separation with dignity at first, accepting that, even though she might not be able to spend her life with Ephed, at least the Bellatani would grow and prosper as a people.

But as it had become apparent with time that no companion was worthy of the *Trachol-ra*, the Belletani had gradually grown to distrust and then to resent the words of their Mystics, and Marni had begun to think about the love she had lost.

The endless stream of new companions that were assigned to Ephed, sometimes as many as one per month by the end, had slowly driven her mad with grief, and she had applied to the Mystics for an early *Mazep-fal*. They had granted it without hesitation, hoping to begin to erase the memory of their mistakes as quickly as possible.

Marni had returned from the *Mazep-fal* as the beautiful twenty-year-old with whom Ephed had first fallen in love. She, of course, no longer remembered her time with Ephed, and by a special decree of the Mystics, no one was ever allowed to speak of their coupling.

Ephed had still seen her occasionally. It was hard to avoid anyone for too long in a village of only 3,000. But to Marni, he was nothing more than he was to everyone else in the tribe, the aging reminder that the gods had either abandoned the Bellatani or were prone to mistakes.

The stream of companions had ended eventually, and Ephed had been left alone and uncertain of his future in the tribe.

After resting on the side of the path for nearly an hour, Ephed had an idea. He walked a short distance from the path to a nearby thicket, searching for a particular—ah! There it was. He spotted a small stand of carbonic reeds, a tubular plant that grew slowly and which had incredible tensile strength, leaching minerals from the soil and incorporating them into its fibrous stem. This particular growth, as it fell along the sacred path, had not been exploited for building materials as most nearer to the Bellatani village had.

He found a rock with a sharp edge and worked at cutting down one of the reeds. When struck at an angle perpendicular to the direction of growth, the fibers snapped cleanly. It was the work of only a few minutes.

Returning to the rock fall with his prize, Ephed found a suitable fulcrum and then wedged the end of the reed under the rock nearest to the edge of the path. Throwing all of his weight onto the reed, he was able to lift the rock out of its self-made depression and roll it off to the side. He repeated the process with the other rocks, taking small breaks between each. As the sun disappeared over the horizon, he removed the last and the largest rock from the path.

Azon barked happily and began walking, stopping after a moment when he did not feel his charge following close behind. The dog turned around and saw Ephed lying in the middle of the path, snoring softly.

Ephed awoke as the sun rose on the fifth day. He had slept awkwardly, not moving from the spot where he had collapsed, and it was an effort to stand up straight. As the sun rose, he saw the pale blue of the Windlas River closer than he had expected. He'd been so intent on his task the previous day that he had not stopped to look ahead.

The Windlas was one of the few features of the path that was spoken of openly among the Bellatani. It was the entire reason that every member of the tribe learned to pilot a raft, even though the closest substantial body of water to their village was more than a day's walk to the south. All of their drinking and irrigation water came from wells, natural springs, and a few rain collectors.

Ephed was surprised to see the river so close. Somehow, with two days largely wasted—one hiding from hail and rain and the other spent clearing the path—he was less than one day behind schedule. If he could make good time to the edge of the Windlas and then make the crossing before the sun set, he would be on track to arrive on sacred ground before the end of the sixth day.

Perhaps the gods were with him on the path after all.

Azon, sensing a change in Ephed's mood, set a brisk pace, and for once, his charge matched him step for step. They covered the miles to the Windlas quickly, and by early afternoon, they stood on the banks of the river.

They approached a small pier. Ephed could see a raft built in the familiar style tied to a post at the end of the wooden walkway. Sticking out of the water near the raft, he could see several carbonic reed poles, each a great deal longer than the one he had used to move the rocks—if the Windlas ran as deep as everyone claimed.

As soon as Ephed stepped onto the pier, Azon left his side and walked a short distance to a small hut made of loosely spaced carbonic reeds with a thatched roof. He entered the hut, laid down, and closed his eyes. Apparently, he would not be joining Ephed on the remainder of his journey.

Ephed approached the raft. The Windlas was wide, so wide that the opposing shore was merely a thick line on the horizon. The current was so slow that Ephed might have assumed he was looking at a lake had he not known better.

The raft was sturdy, made of several thick xapax logs lashed together. The spaces between the logs were sealed with a thick layer of xapax resin. Ephed had smelled the sickly sweet tree sap when he first stepped onto the pier.

He selected what appeared to be the longest carbonic reed and stepped onto the raft. Untying the mooring, he pushed off from the pier. The opposite landing was a slightly raised point on the dark line of the distant shore.

He soon fell into an easy rhythm as he poled the raft, setting a moderate pace that he hoped would get him to his destination before the sun had completely disappeared without exhausting him entirely before he arrived. It took him several minutes to adjust to the cross-current, which was strong despite the still appearance of the water.

The monotony of his actions and his surroundings encouraged a wandering mind, and Ephed found himself, not entirely willingly, thinking of one of the darker periods of his life—the weeks and months following the pronouncement by the Mystics that he was not the true *Trachol-ra.*

They had supported him as long as they could, hoping that, at some point, another child might be conceived by Ephed or by another pair, vindicating their position, but after his sixtieth year had passed, they had decided that the cost of remaining pariahs was simply too high.

Brokering a closed-door deal with the Council, the Mystics had regaining some ceremonial power. They had resumed their duties as caretakers of the path.

Ephed, who had been relying mainly on the Mystics for support by that point, found himself without a single ally. The Council had given up on him long before, and the majority of the Bellatani people had followed their lead. Without the Mystics, Ephed was alone. Most of the tribe-mates he had counted as friends had either gone through the *Mazep-fal* or were ignoring him.

He had moved to an isolated spot on the edge of the village after his first petition to make the *Mazep-fal* had been rejected and built a simple hut of scrap wood. He'd dug his own well and lived off of the land as much as possible. He'd visited the main sections of the village infrequently, his advancing age marking him as the false *Trachol-ra* even for those he had never met and those who no longer remembered him directly.

He had passed into memory on the edge of the village, often referred to by the Bellatani people as more myth than anything else.

Two-thirds of the way across the Windlas River, Ephed stopped poling the raft and laid down on the deck, staring up at the violet sky and wondering if it was really worth the effort to continue on to Endur's Temple beyond the far shore of the Windlas. He would return to the village as a younger man, but to what, exactly, would he be returning?

He lay like that for a long time, thinking about his life and wondering if he would really forget all of it the next day. Did he want to forget it? Would it be better to simply wander off and disappear into history, defeated but still whole, clutching his memories, the one thing that no one but the gods could take away?

A voice he had not heard in years drifted above the surface of the water in the gathering darkness. It was Marni, and she was repeating one of her favorite passages from the Mystic tomes:

"The greatest weakness of man lies in giving up. But inaction is the path to Etnu. The most certain means for success are to trust in Endur and to always try just one more time."

Trust in Endur. Ephed had long abandoned that dictum. But hearing Marni's voice, whether sent by divine channels or entirely imagined, renewed him in a way that the gods never could. He could not stand the thought that somewhere, somehow, she might be disappointed in him, that she would think him a coward, if only in his memories of her.

He set his feet firmly on the deck. He'd kicked his sandals to the side earlier and rubbed the soles of his feet with xapax resin to grip the smooth logs. He lifted the carbonic reed back over the side of the raft and began poling with a new strength. He did not know what would happen when he entered Endur's Temple. He did not know what life would be like if he completed the *Mazep-fal* and returned to the village. But he would not give up. He would complete his journey.

He fought through the night to make up the distance he had drifted and reach the pier on the far side of the Windlas. When he finally lashed the raft and stepped, once more, onto solid ground, the western horizon was beginning to glow. The sun would rise on the sixth day in less than an hour.

Ephed stumbled forward, barely able to keep his spent legs underneath him. He needed to rest. He sat down under a large tree and leaned against the trunk, intending to resume his journey after a few moments. Within seconds, he was asleep.

He never heard the approaching footsteps.

When Ephed awoke, he could tell by the sun that he had slept for more than half of the day. He did not know how far Endur's Temple was from the Windlas, but unless it was very close, he would never reach it before the sun set. He would not make the *Mazep-fal* in six days.

He was surprised by how little he cared. His renewed purpose from the night before had evaporated as he slept, and he wondered again whether it was worth the effort.

Would completing the *Mazep-fal* erase the hard feelings? Would proving that he was a true member of the tribe and not some type of dark prophet sent by Etnu make a difference? Or would he simply return as a younger man to a tribe that, at best, was indifferent of him, unable to remember the hardships of the past decades and uncertain why his tribe-mates continued to shun him. Did he really want to go through the slow process of learning to live in isolation again?

"I take it that you are Ephed?" said a deep voice.

Ephed, startled out of his melancholy thoughts, jumped up and spun around to face the voice. A man sat on a large rock several feet behind the tree against which Ephed had been leaning. His close-cropped hair was a brilliant orange, tinged with grey, and he wore the dusty green robes of a Mystic.

"My apologies. I did not mean to startle you. My name is Ligrif," said the man.

"Who are you? Why are you hear?" asked Ephed.

"I am the *Xenro*, the one who waits. I remain here, on the banks of the Windlas, to guide pilgrims on the last portion of their journey to Endur's Temple. And when they return, after the rebirth, I point them home."

"No one told me there would be a Mystic here," said Ephed.

"The position of *Xenro* is not shared with the public. You might be surprised at how many secrets our order possesses," said Ligrif. His eyes sparkled in the late afternoon sun.

"How do you know my name?" asked Ephed.

"A pair of high priests visited me not long ago. They told me that you might be coming, though they did not think it likely that you would make it this far. The path is not meant for old men."

"And what did they tell you to do if I did make it this far?" asked Ephed.

Ligrif shrugged and looked away. He drummed his fingers on the scabbard of a knife he held in his lap.

"So that's why they granted me access to the path," said Ephed.

"Peace," said Ligrif. "I will not harm you."

"Won't Endur be disappointed?" said Ephed, looking around for a rock or other implement he might be able to use to defend himself.

"The high priests may be disappointed, but Endur? I find it unlikely. I have seen far less worthy men than you complete the *Mazep-fal*. We are all the same in his eyes. No, I decided shortly after my visitors left that if Endur did not want you here, he would have stopped you himself. Either we are all deserving of life or none of us are."

"So you will let me pass?" asked Ephed.

"Yes. Though I would not recommend leaving until tomorrow. The remainder of the path is short, but it would be treacherous to cross in the dark," said Ligrif.

"I'm already at the end of my sixth day," said Ephed

Ligrif chuckled and climbed down from his perch, turning to walk towards a hut a short distance away. As he walked, he said over his shoulder, "Endur does not trouble himself with the timeframes of man. You are not the first to exceed the six-day rule, and you will not be the last."

Ephed hurried after the Mystic, and for the first time he looked to the east. A great dome rose from the rocky terrain beyond the Windlas. It must have been at least thirty miles away, but it still dominated the horizon. It was low, with a gentle curvature so that if it were a complete circle, the vast bulk of it would need to lie underground.

Endur's Temple. A massive structure built by the gods themselves. No one could ever remember it, though if they had been able, it was unlikely that anyone would have been able to describe it adequately. Ephed understood why Azon had stayed behind on the other side of the Windlas. He would no longer need a guide to find his destination.

Ephed followed Ligrif to his hut. It appeared, from the outside, to be tiny, but as he entered, he immediately faced a set of stairs that descended sharply.

Ligrif turned at the bottom of the stairs and beckoned, "Come in. Come in. You can see what I and the other *Xenros* have spent the last ten thousand years building. We switch off every twenty years, you know. He will be along three summers from now, and I will be off the see Endur, just like you."

The air was heavy with the bitter smell of burning xapax resin. Several lanterns hung from the ceiling. Shadows flickered in and out of existence as the lanterns danced in the breeze created by the opening and closing of the door.

The main room was several times the size of the hut as it had appeared from the outside. The walls were bare soil, though they had been compacted and smoothed by a practiced hand and looked like polished stone. Groupings of carbonic reeds supported the ceiling, connected to each other by a network of xapax wood beams. The floor was covered with rough-hewn xapax planks.

Shelves covered one wall, filled with the handwritten texts of the Mystics. Despite the size of the room, it was almost entirely unfurnished. Aside from the shelves, there was a single table with two chairs and a mat on the floor with an open book lying to one side.

Two doorways led off to unlit spaces on opposite ends of the main room. Ligrif gestured to one, "You will sleep there tonight. There is a lantern just inside the doorway. Light it if you wish, and then sleep. Tomorrow, you shall meet Endur."

He turned and entered the opposite room, leaving the lanterns lit in the main area. Ephed entered his room and collapsed onto the mat inside. Despite already having slept for most of the day, he was asleep again in an instant.

Ephed awoke to a terrible wailing. It took him a moment to remember where he was and a moment longer to recognize the voice. Ligrif was greeting the morning with a Mystic chant.

He climbed the stairs, opened the door, and was greeted by a blazing sun that was already well above the horizon.

Ligrif finished his chant and turned to Ephed, "Ah, you are awake. Good. I delayed my morning rituals for as long as possible to allow you to sleep. You will need your strength."

"Do you have anything that I could eat?" asked Ephed. For the first time on his trip, he was aware of his stomach.

"You know as well as I that pilgrims may only eat what they carry with them," said Ligrif.

"Yes, but I just thought—" began Ephed.

"You thought that since the six-day rule can be broken," said Ligrif, turning back to the rising sun and bowing deeply, "that all rules of the *Mazep-fal* are equally unimportant. It is true that my order enforces many conventions that are of no real consequence. But this is not one of them. The process of rebirth is not gentle."

"I should be on my way, then," said Ephed.

"Yes, *Trachol-ra*, you should."

The sun had begun to descend, and Ephed guessed that he was still more than ten miles from Endur's Temple. The low dome now dominated his vision. He could no longer distinctly make out its ends as it stretched north and south.

The surface of the temple, which he had originally thought to be smooth and polished stone, now appeared uneven and craggy, as though the peak of a great, rounded mountain had begun to force its way up and out of the soil.

He was tempted to stare at the temple as he walked, marveling at its scale, but the uneven ground made it impossible. Ligrif had not exaggerated about the difficult of this last length of the path. If he lifted his eyes for too long, he would risk tripping on the uneven and rocky ground.

There was no clear path to follow, no soft surfaces that might show the way his tribe-mates had used before him. He walked as quickly as he could, and the doubts and fears of the previous days melted away in the hot sun. Being here, actually standing on the hallowed ground and seeing the massive temple, had restored Ephed's faith.

Ligrif had been right. If Endur did not want him here, he would have stopped him on the path. If he was not worthy, he would never have made it this far. He would be a true Belletani soon, and he realized that he had never wanted anything in life more than the embrace of his god.

Now within only a mile or two of the temple, Ephed paused. The sun was beginning to set over the temple from his perspective, and its façade was becoming a silhouette on the cloud-streaked sky. He strained his eyes to find the massive door on the side of the temple towards which he was heading. Over it, he could just make out the words "Endur's Temple," carved in mammoth letters in the ancient language of the gods:

ENDURANCE.

He pressed on, and soon he stood mere paces away from the entrance to the home of his creator. His heartbeat quickened, and he stepped over the threshold.

It was dark in the temple. The only light was what little spilled in from outside as the twilight deepened. Ephed took several uncertain steps forward, probing with his feet to keep from stumbling.

He continued on slowly for several minutes. The open door was a rapidly diminishing square of light behind him. He saw nothing but could tell that he was in a vast chamber as each tentative footstep echoed against distant walls. The floor was smooth, and he never once stumbled. It was also cold, unnaturally so. He could feel the heat being drawn out of the soles of his feet through his sandals with every step.

A light appeared in the distance. He could not tell how far away it was, but he turned slightly and headed towards it as quickly as he felt he could in the darkness. He walked for several minutes, the light never appearing to grow larger or brighter.

Then it disappeared.

Startled, Ephed stumbled forward, and his outstretched hand hit a smooth wall just a few feet in front of him. He paused to catch his breath, leaning forward against the wall, which promptly dissolved.

He fell into a blinding white light. He struggled back to his feet, and after his eyes adjusted, he looked at his surroundings. He was in a large chamber with smooth, white walls. Every inch was lit from an unseen source by pure, brilliant light. It was entirely empty.

"Welcome to *Endurance.* Please state your name."

He nearly fainted. The voice of Endur, if that was who had spoken, seemed to come from everywhere at once. He was caught off guard by the use of old tongue, and he struggled to form a response.

"My...name...is Ephed Biral...of the Bellatani."

"The name Ephed Biral is not recognized. Please state your name," the tone of the voice remained the same.

Not recognized? Endur did not know who he was? He was the *Trachol-ra*! He had prepared himself for the worst, but he had not anticipated indifference.

Ephed panicked and said the first thing that he could think of in what little of the old tongue he could remember, "I am the...son...of Nikan and Madrelass Biral."

"Scanning."

The word was entirely unfamiliar to Ephed. He tried to think back to his early days, to his schooling, to find a meaning. His thoughts were interrupted by a bright flash.

"Identity confirmed by DNA analysis. The human population has recovered from the effects of suspended animation and has produced viable offspring. Phase one of colonization complete. DNA rejuvenation suspended. The *Endurance* will return to Earth to begin phase two."

Ephed, again unable to understand the voice, feared the worst. He stood for a moment longer, waiting some further instruction. The bright light in the room dimmed slightly, and the floor began to vibrate. Ephed's faith failed him, and he turned and ran. The doorway leading back to the large, dark chamber was still open, and he sprinted as quickly as his old legs could manage through the darkness.

As he ran towards the exit, it appeared to recede. He realized after a moment that it wasn't shrinking or getting further away. It was closing. He increased his pace and felt his heart pounding against his ribs as tears flowed down his cheeks. He was not worthy. Endur had not granted him new life. He did not know what would happen once the temple sealed itself, and he did not want to find out.

When he reached the massive entranceway, the opening was only slightly taller than him. He ducked involuntarily as he passed under the slowly descending slab and tripped on the threshold, falling on the rocky ground. The door closed behind him with a massive, reverberating thud.

The Temple of Endur threw off the dust of thirty thousand years and ascended, silent except for the sound of falling rocks and a deep, rhythmic pulsing.

Ephed lay on his back and watched as the great circle of the temple, its outer edge illuminated by a strange green glow, rose higher and higher into the sky and then disappeared into the night sky. Ω

Enjoying the first issue?

News & Announcements
Articles
Reviews
Podcasts
"Best of" Lists

There's more great content on NonlocalSciFi.com!

And be sure to follow us on social media
so you never miss a thing!

Us and Everybody Else

Written By
Valery Amborski

A teeming office. A raucous of noise, like an off-key orchestra. The visual telecommunication systems never quiet, their screens constantly switching on and off, clicking and buzzing and ringing. The meaningless chatter shared over cubicle walls, increasingly distracting. The elevator dings. The fax machines hum and clank. My supervisor stands, arms crossed, in the corner. The broken rhythm of well-polished shoes tapping on an unpolished floor. The clicking, the buzzing, the ringing, the humming, the clanking. A procedurally disconcerting soundtrack to my programmed nine-to-five.

Ever menacingly, the towering stack of should-be-obsolete paperwork on the desk in front of me increases by the second. Volumes of information that should have been catalogued electronically from the start land on my desk instead. The Earth is governed by electronics, and still people do not trust the computers. I glance repeatedly at the clock in utter disbelief of its astonishing lack of speed.

In my body's feeble attempt to preserve my sanity, the chaotic ambience of the bustling office around me is muted. Their mouths move but produce no sound. The screens flash on and off but do not click. All I can hear is the sound of the second hand traveling too slow between each notch on the clock face.

Tick. And the eventual tock.

At this point, I'm not even sure whose side my own body is on. Against my better judgment, I tune back into reality just in time for the clock to strike one as my supervisor adds a fresh pile of contracts on top of the existing paper tower. The swelling heap of contracts, looming over my seemingly shrinking self-consciousness; my supervisor, looming over my lowering self confidence. Taunting me, the mountain of printed legal jargon creates a visual manifestation of my unhappiness. Not only for this job, but for my life as a whole. I have been trapped in this office for ages, working a job that I hate, to support a wife that I hate, in a world that hates me. All of this proving to be an unsuccessful attempt at filling the void of loneliness that I am left with without you.

I am but a worker bee, lost in the queen's hive. I am suffocating slowly.

I skim over the fine print that litters each lengthy page. The formal business contracts infect the smooth, white papers like a disease. Paper that should be used for something far superior. Something more meaningful, more personal, more poetic. Smothering my sudden discontent with the corporate world in which I have forever imprisoned myself, I mechanically work through the stack of papers. Trying hard not to look at the clock every three minutes, I am a drone, programmed only to read and sign, read and sign.

Struggling only to read and sign.

At last, that damned clock reaches the long awaited hour of five. I calmly place my pen back in its charging station, return the stack of completed paperwork, swipe my wrist through the time card reader, descend six floors down the elevator. It is a fifteen minute drive before I reach my neighborhood. As I pull into my driveway, I am comforted by the fact that it will only be a short time now before I can truly relax. Before I can see you again. I can truly be happy, if only for a moment.

I enter the house to my wife complaining about the leaking bathroom sink that has needed to be fixed for the past two weeks. Her blonde hair is tied in a messy knot at the top of her head. In some faint capacity I love her, but all she ever does is bitch. There is a disorganized pile of unpaid bills and loan applications on the kitchen counter, a red "Final Notice" stamp displayed on far too many of them, like blood smeared across pure white bed sheets at a murder scene.

This room is where we are supposed to make our meals and enjoy them together as a family. But she doesn't cook anymore, and I don't know how. A button on the wall to my left reveals the refrigerator, and I grab a bottle of carbonated gluco-hydrate. I explain to my darling wife that I had a *very* long day at work and that I just need a few moments to myself to wind down and relax. I suggest, light heartedly, that she do the same. Visually defeated, she either understands or gives up.

When I finally escape into the basement, the floor cold on my bare feet, I am pleased to find that the MRG is fully charged. I allow myself a moment of praise for remembering to plug the machine in after my previous session. I have been looking forward to this, longing for this, all day. This is the closest to true home that I have felt in a very, very long time. The chair looks inviting as I advance to the station and strap myself in. The coolness of the leather straps is refreshing against my warm ankles.

As the power sphere's blue fluorescents cast a cool glow over my skin, I type in the serial number for the specific point to which I wish to remember. I roll up my sleeve and plug the cable into the matching port installed in my forearm. I lean my head against the back of the chair and close my eyes. It only takes a moment before my mind is transported to the only place where I ever want to be. The only place where I ever feel happy. The only place where I can be with you.

I am at the waterfront, sitting on a thick, yellowish tree trunk that had at some point been washed ashore. The bark has disappeared entirely, creating a smooth, wooden place for us to sit. It is after midnight. The full moon illuminates the beach like a night light, creating deep shadows between the rocks and water-logged tree limbs that line the coast behind us. The slow breeze is cold on my skin as it travels over the water to the beach.

Your long, smooth, crimson curls dance like the waves as they crash and vanish in the sand. I wish, as I have many times before, that I had had a jacket to offer you, to layer over your own, so you wouldn't be so cold. So you could stop shivering so much. The clear, navy blue sky reveals the distant stars that twinkle, just like your eyes as they meet mine, reflecting our moonlit environment.

"It's just us and everybody else," I say as I run my hand down the side of your cheek. My hands tremble, falling victim to my nervous system, as I stare into your beautiful, loving eyes. I could stare into those eyes for an eternity.

I wish that life could stay like this forever. It is becoming apparent how much you are shivering, so I open my own jacket to let you in. After too short a moment, you stand up as though you are ready to leave. There is something about your eyes that isn't quite right, something unfamiliar as you seem to be looking through me.

The horizon begins to lighten, and my surroundings begin to flicker. Our time is almost up. A few more gusts of wind and a cycle of crashing waves, and I begin to fade back into reality. Just in time to miss your heart stop. Just in time to miss your body slouch onto the sand. Just in time to miss the ambulance try to rescue your lifeless body, and I am left here forever, only with the memory of you. Ω

Shoot the Devil

Written By
Nicholas C. Rossis

"*Papieren,*" a voice barked behind me.

I froze in my tracks. I thought I could sneak into my destination unseen at this late hour, but this city had more eyes than cobblestones. *Act natural,* my instructor's voice whispered in my head. The same thing he had repeated daily during six months of ceaseless training.

I turned around slowly, one hand in the air, the other digging into my pocket for my battered wallet. Since leather was no longer used in the twenty-second century, this was an heirloom brought along specifically for the purpose. I fished out my pass to hand it over to the impatient hand.

A second guard was looking on, a bored look on his face. *God, they're so young,* I thought. The countless hours spent training had not prepared me for the stark reality of Nazi Germany. Somehow, I had expected everything to be more cinematic and less...well, less real. That's the problem with time travel; everything is so similar, yet the smallest detail can seem odd.

I examined the soldier while he studied my pass, his gaze shooting from my face to the folded piece of paper and back. His uniform smelled of wet wool, and I caught a hint of grease from the menacing machinegun hanging leisurely from his shoulder. A sweeter smell—Brilliantine?—wafted from his head, startling me. I stared at his iron helmet, my eyes catching on the twin lightning bolts stenciled on its side. A silver pair on his collar mirrored them, glinting under the faint glow of the streetlight. I wondered if they were made out of real silver and fought a sudden urge to reach out and rub them with my fingers.

"Come on," the second guard said in German, shooting an impatient glance at the clock sitting atop the bell tower in the square's middle. This one's insignia was dark grey, and I tried in vain to remember what, if anything, that meant.

The first guard hesitated for a moment before handing me my papers. "Where do you live?" he asked me.

I nodded with my jaw towards the aging building around the corner, where, according to my papers, I had lived for the past three years. I tried to keep my words to a minimum. The endless hours spent practicing my accent notwithstanding, I did not want to take any chances.

He studied me for a moment, and I forced myself to meet his eyes, hoping they did not reflect my terror.

"Go," he said in the end.

I nodded and turned slowly away, my boots scuffing and kicking at the cobbles in what I hoped was a display of worry-free indifference. Only after I had turned the corner did I let myself exhale, leaning against a door frame until my knees stopped shaking.

I pulled out a skeleton key and jiggled it into a rusted lock. It clicked softly, and I hurried inside the medieval building, shutting the door behind me as I slipped into a dark corridor, filled with the reassuring stench of boiled cabbage. A baby's plaintive cries attacked me from an apartment to my left, followed by a faint argument. I pulled out a dull grey metal cylinder from a hidden pocket in my thick coat. It hissed when I pried it open and expanded to become a two-barreled gun. With a soft whir, a laser sight snapped in place at the top, projecting a red dot on the wall across from me.

Its comforting weight in my hand helped to slow my breathing. I started up the narrow steps, but a brown door creaked open and revealed a woman's ancient face. She threw me a stern, suspicious look as I squeezed the weapon into my pocket.

"Who are you?" she asked me in German, glancing at the bulge under my coat.

"A friend..." I rasped and coughed to clear my clogged throat. "A friend of Dr. Schumann's. He's visiting family in Berlin."

My heart pounded as she took this in, her eyes never leaving my face. Finally, she shot me a venomous look. "Tell him he's late for the rent."

"I will," I promised.

Without a word, she slammed the door, and I wiped beads of sweat from my brow as I made my way into Dr. Schumann's apartment.

I slinked inside, wrinkling my nose; the apartment reeked of alcohol. I blinked for a moment before moving any further, my eyes getting used to the low light.

"Greetings, doctor," I said to a still silhouette on an armchair while hanging my coat on a nail by the door.

There was no reply. As my intel suggested, Dr. Schumann lay in his favorite corner of the room, dead as a lanky doornail, the victim of chronic liver failure. His half-open eyes reflected the soft light coming from outside through the dingy, tattered curtains. I padded over to close them, avoiding his lifeless stare until I had closed his eyes.

The soft music coming from the huge radio facing him came to an abrupt end, followed by the shouts of an announcer. As my heart skipped a beat, I wondered if I should keep it on, but I decided that my nerves were too fraught for sudden sounds. I turned the knob, welcoming the ensuing quiet.

A thin beam of pale light cut through the middle of the tall window overlooking the small plaza where he would arrive in less than an hour. As I headed towards it, I tripped over an empty bottle and kneeled to plonk it onto a table.

I considered turning on a light as I pried the window open to glance outside. Chances were no one was looking up, but I had already maxed out my luck for one night, and I did not want to take any risks. Pulling a nearby chair to the window, I drew my gun to examine it under the streetlamp's soft glow. The laser sight whirred and turned as it calculated distance, a red dot pointing at the ceiling.

I lost track of time staring at the twin barrels until a car sped into the plaza and four dark-clad men jumped out and silently scanned the darkened street. I instinctively drew back into the room's shadows as they studied the surrounding buildings. After a moment, they disappeared, moving towards the plaza's four corners, while the driver parked the car under my building.

It won't be long now.

I rubbed sweat off of my palms and pulled a pair of gloves from my pocket. The last thing I wanted was to have the gun slip through my fingers as I pulled the trigger; I only had one chance at this. I stared with disdain at my sweaty, shaking fingers as I pushed them into their soft constraints.

The sound of more cars screeching outside made me hurry. I snapped the gloves onto my hands. I stole a look outside; three cars had stopped in front of the entrance of the city hall. I had no idea what the Fuehrer wanted there at this late hour; my intel did not extend that far. Nor did I need to know, of course. Like countless Jews before me, all I wanted was a shot at the man who had nearly destroyed my people.

With a flick of my thumb, I switched the laser off and stared down the sight, focusing on the car in the middle. I almost slammed the trigger as its door flew open and a bodyguard stepped out to glance around, but I forced myself to stand still, any sudden movement certain to draw attention to me. When the man stepped to the side, holding the door open, I had him in my sights.

The monster who had been responsible for millions of deaths sprang out of the car with an agility that caught me off guard. I cursed silently, flicking the laser sight on with my thumb. A tiny red dot, clearly visible through the laser sight, danced on the stone steps, trying to lock onto the short man rushing towards the yawning doors of the building.

Realizing that in a few seconds he would disappear through them, I panicked, and my finger twitched. The bullet exploded against one of the columns adorning the building's entrance, sending a rain of stone splinters against the startled men.

Shit!

I drew a deep breath, trying to slow down my pounding heart. I squeezed the trigger a second time, just as the Fuehrer spun around to face me. His moustached lip quivered as he stared at me, bug-eyed.

His head exploded into countless tiny fragments, spraying warm droplets onto his stunned bodyguards. Blood flew onto the steps below like swirling, scarlet raindrops, baptizing the marble in his blood, as the Fuehrer's knees buckled, sending his body to crash against the stone.

Loud yells and shouts shot from outside. A woman screamed as I brought my hand to my mouth to drown a cackle, pulling back into the safety of the dark apartment.

I did it!

My heart filled with a primal joy as my pulse pounded on my temples. A countdown started in my head; I had to let Zion know I had succeeded. Rotating the buckle on my belt to reveal a small indentation, I clicked it with my finger. The buckle split open, and I pressed the inconspicuous button inside before releasing the breath that had caught in my throat.

Within a few seconds, an agent would travel back in time to stop me from entering the time machine, thus undoing the assassination. It did not matter; I had succeeded. Even better, I had the recording on my weapon, protected by a weak paradox field, to prove it. I shut my eyelids as the room started to spin and fade away.

When I cracked them open again, I was in the middle of a sparsely decorated room, lying down on a silky chair. A warm light filled the white room and revealed my instructor's smiling face. He stepped out from behind an undersized desk with nothing but a glowing, transparent screen on top.

"Congratulations, son, you did it," he said and palmed my shoulder. I looked up at him, a wide grin on my face. He wore his usual khakis, a blue beret sticking from his right shoulder strap.

"Thank you," I said. "It's a pity he can't stay dead."

He lifted his broad shoulders. "You know we can't change the course of history. By stopping you before you enter the time stream, we prevent that from happening. Only after you've had your fun, though."

I had to laugh; the man was right. I had had a great time killing Hitler.

"But they let JFK stay dead," I complained, not for the first time.

"You know that's different. That prevented a nuclear war."

I scoffed but did not insist; I was too exhilarated for that. "Now what?" I asked him, and his smile disappeared, his face turning serious. I mirrored his expression as he handed me my own blue beret.

"Now you're one of us," he said. "Wear it with pride."

Tears welled up in my eyes as my fingers caressed the soft fabric. "I will," I promised and rushed to my feet. A wave of nausea crashed over me, sending me back onto the chair.

"Easy now," my instructor said. "You just came back. Give it a minute."

I nodded and allowed him to help me to my feet after a moment. "Are you coming?"

"And miss all this paperwork?" He nodded towards the screen on the desk.

I shook his hand. "Thank you. For everything."

His amber eyes studied me. "Was it all you hoped it would be?"

I never knew my grin could grow even wider. "And more."

I staggered to the door.

"I'll catch you later," he said as he slumped behind the desk.

The door hissed open, and I waved my thanks. I stepped outside on unsteady legs, almost crashing into a nurse.

"Easy there," he said, jumping back.

"I'm sorry, I'm just back—"

"From assassinating Hitler, I know." He pointed at a sign outside the room with the words *Post-Mission Recovery Room*. His eyes met mine, and he opened his mouth but hesitated. "Can I..." he stammered.

I raised my eyebrows and waited.

"Mind if I ask you something?" he finally blurted out.

"Sure." I leaned with my back on the wall.

"Oh, I'm sorry, are you still recovering?"

"No, I'm fine," I assured him. "Just catching my breath. What did you want to know?"

He pursed his lips. "Why do you do it?"

"Excuse me?"

He cocked his head to examine me. "I don't get it. Thousands of people travelling back in time to kill Hitler when you all know you can't really change anything. What's the point?"

A realization hit me, and my lips curled upwards. "You're not Jewish, are you?"

He shook his head. "No, Arab."

"What's your name?"

"I'm sorry, where are my manners?" He extended his hand. "I'm Hasan."

I squeezed his fingers. "Have you made your Hajj yet, Hasan?"

His face beamed. "Yes. I went last year."

"Did you perform the stoning of the devil?"

"*Ramy al-Jamarat?* Of course."

"Can you describe it for me?"

He shrugged. "We throw stones at the devil, to remember Abraham's defiance of him."

"Does that hurt the devil?"

A soft laugh escaped Hasan's lips. "I guess not."

"Well, our devil walked this earth, so we don't throw pebbles at him. We fire bullets."

"I..." His voice trailed and he chuckled. "I think I understand. Thank you." He frowned as a siren blared above us. "I'm sorry, I have to go. We have another assassination in five minutes." He rushed off, waving his goodbyes.

"No problem."

Placing my new beret on my head, I watched him disappear into a lift. He waved at me one last time as the doors slid shut.

I shut my eyes, and the image of Hitler's head exploding filled my mind. Yes, it was everything I had dreamed it would be. I wished I was allowed to relive the experience of killing him, but I consoled myself with the thought that nothing could top that experience. Then a wide grin crept onto my face as I remembered my appointment with the Roman Department next week. In six months' time, once my training was complete, Lucius Flavius Silva would be met with more than Zealots in Masada...Ω

Catalyst

Written By
Aaron Hamilton

Cribbs tried not to think of how lucky they'd been, afraid he would somehow cause the scales to tip back against them. He hadn't stopped to question it when his cell door had slid open, when his impounded ship had been released from grav-lock, or even when they had escaped without pursuit. His cynicism resurfaced as his pulse slowed.

"I'll leave the 'how' for later. Just tell me why you betrayed Mogidu and freed me," he muttered as he checked scans once again for enemy craft. Thellia turned in the chair to face him, and his icy calm sublimated away. The last copilot he had worked with was long gone, and he could hardly picture the last woman he'd had aboard his ship.

"Mogidu's a man no one should have to endure, including me. I wanted out, just like you, and I saw my chance." Her eyes were nearly as dark as the void outside the cockpit, and they held at once sensual promise and the pity he had sensed while still Mogidu's prisoner. "Is being rescued by the heroine too much for your ego?" Her lopsided smile nearly disarmed him.

"I...look, I don't really care. I'm just curious. Things went too well. We should be taking fire from several of Mogidu's fighters by now. We never should've made it off the ground." The muscles of his jaw bunched as he squinted at the instruments again.

She leaned slightly toward him over the arm of the chair. The pendant nestled between her breasts nearly distracted him from the view of her body. When he looked up to meet her eyes, she smiled playfully while she covered the pendant with her hand. A turn of her head brought long black hair over her shoulder to obscure the milky jewel.

"You stole it and needed to get out of Mogidu's domain fast," Cribbs snarled. "Who better to help you than a man as desperate as me?"

"Come now, Cribbs. Don't spoil this. I was counting on Mogidu's men to steal it, and you stole it from them. They caught you and felt you would make a fine example to anyone else who might think to cross them. I suppose it was going to be your last big score before you retired your aging body somewhere quiet and warm." She smiled at that, he assumed because she couldn't imagine him going legit. "Would you believe me if I told you it's finally in the hands of its rightful protector? Besides, I'll give you more than your freedom. You'll never have to watch over your shoulder for Mogidu or worry someone else will cash you in for the Hegemony's impressive bounty."

She stood and approached him from behind his seat. He faced front, not wanting to admit the difficulty of keeping his eyes from her. A palm brushed lightly over his chest as curled fingers brushed his cheek.

"Your name will live forever as the hero who defied two of the fiercest enemies a man could have."

Confined in Mogidu's archaic cellblock, when Cribbs had let himself stop worrying about the tortures in store for him, his mind had turned to Thellia. He had heard rumors of Mogidu's consort, unrivaled in her beauty, accomplice in the crime lord's legendary cruelties, and her hypnotic stare. In his youth, Cribbs had stolen his share of hearts as well as treasures, but none had ever entranced him like Thellia. More importantly, her hold on Mogidu was no exaggeration, and she had used it to free them both. The light dancing on the jewel broke her spell, returned Cribbs to his present dilemma.

"Where do you figure there won't be somebody who wants the Hegemony's money? Hell, maybe that's how you're going to finance your independence from Mogidu."

"Sell you out?" Her breath caressed his left ear, stopping him before he could spin his chair. "Oh, I've got a plan, but it can't succeed without you and your ship. We're in this together."

Together, the word pulled at something deep in his gut, inviting and unsettling.

"And when we've arrived wherever these coordinates lie, my use will be at an end. This isn't the first time I've been used, lady." The control stick protested as he squeezed it in his fist. The pain in his knuckles focused him.

"You insult me, Cribbs. As if I could look into that baby face of yours and lie to you."

Cribbs had to admit, she was a good actress, and it had probably kept her alive during Mogidu's renowned rages. "No man with a heart like yours deserves to be hunted, tormented, caged—not when your freedom can serve so great a purpose."

"How long can that freedom last?" He stretched forward and felt the holster secured under the pilot console, slid his fingers across it until the familiar grip welcomed his palm. She spun the chair to face her, but he was thrown back too quickly to grab the weapon. She flipped up the arm rests, swung her leg over his, and straddled him.

"Freedom my family can reward. My army can enforce it, and I can fill it with happiness."

Her lips locked onto his, and his plans for her quickly changed. She smelled of Tzarzt dust and tasted of Shyl spirits. A low moan escaped her as she tugged at his belt. How many times had he dared to imagine the heat of her against him? He lifted her as he stood, stumbling a bit as she clung to him. Wrapped in strong legs, he made his way to a bunk, her fingers snaking through his hair. She rolled on top of him and shed her dress in one liquid movement. Her black eyes pulled at him, and he might have drowned if not for the swaying of the jewel above him.

The blaring alarm found him confused, still exhausted, and tangled in her dress. She reacted more quickly and found the pilot's chair before he could hop into his pants. She bent naked over the keys, tapping frantically.

"Your worries were justified, of course. It was only a matter of time." The pendant swung beneath her face, nearly touching the keys.

Cribbs cringed as he realized that twenty years ago he would have been distracted by her nudity. Now all he felt was his mortality as he slammed down into the copilot's chair to confront his fears.

"Mogidu? The Hegemony?"

"Both, if you can believe it. Mogidu is closer." The screens confirmed her estimate.

"The Hegemony won't slow down if he's in the way. He's too smart to start anything with them." Cribbs normally wouldn't bet against Mogidu, but the Hegemony's supremacy brooked no dispute.

"He wants the jewel, and he'd risk the Hegemony for it. He won't be disappointed to have us under his boot again either."

"We'll outrun him." Cribbs squeezed the control stick and braced himself in his seat.

"No."

"I'll power up the beams and atomize him." He snapped a switch above his head, but her fingers closed painfully around his wrist."

"We can fight them all, but not that way."

"How?"

"We're almost there."

"I hope so. The engines have been abused past tolerance."

The ship slowed on auto-pilot as they reached the designated coordinates. Cribbs started to ask Thellia what her plan was, but his voice caught in his throat as he turned to face her. A light shone from the jewel, no, from behind the jewel, inside her chest. The cabin brightened almost painfully, and she fell on him the instant he gained his feet. Her grip felt painfully cold, like his blood gradually freezing, working up his arm and into his chest.

"We won't need engines or guns or beams."

She gripped him until he thought his back would snap in her embrace. Soft curves were just illusions. He writhed under spikes of pain in his ribs and gut and groin. The ship shuddered.

"Do you know what horrors Mogidu would unleash with this power? Can you imagine a single free thought in a universe where the Hegemony wielded this?" The jewel's glow pulsed with her breath.

"No," he croaked, not an answer but a plea.

Her lips clamped over his as something thudded into the ship, and a sharp scraping told him that Mogidu had breached the hull. A solitary instant of warmth washed through him, as if they still lay twined in bed, before the cold savagely thrust down his throat and choked his scream.

Crushed against Thellia, Cribbs saw Mogidu enter the cabin behind her. The crime lord grimaced against the white light pouring out to flood the cabin. Mogidu's eyes widened. His eyelids peeled back; then his hair and whole face gave way in a shriek of anguish and despair.

The hull ruptured, and the fierce light spewed Cribbs, the woman, and the meager contents of his ship into the vacuum. Why wasn't he dead? Where was the cold? Why was she giggling as they rushed toward an ocean veiled beneath swirling clouds?

He realized the laughter was just as much his.

"Your name will be immortal, and your children will spread to every corner of the galaxy," her voice boomed inside his head. "The Hegemony will crumble before them and every being will know they owe their freedom to you, to us."

The light seared them a moment after their impact launched the sea into the heavens. The spout grew, and the waters churned, and a million, billion voices sang their farewells as the promised army spilled into space.

Cribbs saw the future, and he felt no fear. Ω

The Assistant Assistant Port Keeper

Written By
Jim Rudnick

Jinni wailed, and when the Assistant Assistant Port Keeper looked at her cage, he could see her back sail standing straight up.

"Leudies again," he said to himself as he tried not to give in to the frustration he felt every time they landed.

Out on the port tarmac, he could see the faint glow growing on Pad 23. They'd made good time coming down from orbit once they'd gotten the automatic okay and landing pad assignment, but then, Leudies always made good time, another reason they were good traders.

Now that gold glow was turning a deeper red, and he could hear the growing sound of their thrusters in the atmosphere. At least they hadn't come down on antimatter pulses. They'd been known to lift off on such and had paid dear penalties the next time they had landed, though Wiggins admitted that that had been almost one Sol year ago. And they sure didn't like paying any landing penalties.

He gathered up the forms that they'd have to fill in on their landing here on Juno.

Out on the tarmac, Customs and Health were going out on the scooter to check cargo manifests. Behind them, an empty transport with offloaders chugged out to receive the cargo—if it was allowed.

"Hmmmph," Wiggins thought. "Leudies always got their cargo in and make good credits, deal after deal."

A trading race, the Leudies worked at making deals all across the Rim, from UrPoPo almost eighty light years distant to Randi. They traded for one thing on one planet, moved to where it was badly needed, and drew a hard bargain with the needy, making credits on both ends.

"But sometimes," Wiggins thought with a smile, "they don't do so well."

Even though they were not well liked, they usually made a profit. And it didn't matter at whose expense they made it. That Crux Epidermis plague of two years ago had come from inward and had threatened to eat away the skin of every Rim citizen it found, and the Leudies had moved the latest serum more than 300 light years at quite a cost to themselves both in energy and lost time. They had been able to get the serum to all who'd needed it on time at a fair profit. Course, then they'd made a much bigger fatter profit on what had happened next.

Every patient, no matter the species, who had used the serum broke down shortly afterward with a full depression, induced, it was said, by chemical changes in the blood–or what passed for blood in certain species–caused by that serum.

The Leudies had also bought the rights for the anti-serum you then had to take to get rid of the depression caused by the original cure. They had made a fortune on that, far more than on the original serum, and of course, they'd never told anyone about the side effects.

Leudies were not liked much nor respected much. Wiggins heard the sound of their boots climbing the three stairs to the Port Keeper's office. Glancing at Jinni, he could see she had wrapped herself up in a ball after trying to dig under her nest in the corner of the cage. Something about Leudies made her react that way every time one came into the Port Keeper's offices, and he wondered, not for the first time, if he should look up the reason later.

He put on a bland smile, squared around his simple uniform shirt, and faced the door, paperwork in hand.

"Right, we're here and we're not paying these exorbitant fees," the first Leudie through the door stated loudly as his cloak brushed the doorsill and he moved in towards the counter.

Wiggins could tell by the forest green of that cloak that this was the captain. He was tall for a Leudie, almost two meters, and built as solidly as they all were. On his head rode the captain's toque that was usual attire for a trader, the captain's double gold bars polished and bright. On his legs, he wore what could only be described as some kind of leggings–thin flesh-hugging green pants that they all wore. On his chest, beneath the green cloak, Wiggins could see a brass-colored shirt. Leudies were humanoids, but they were a more colorful bunch then most.

"Never," said the first mate, who had followed his captain in tandem and who also wore the Leudie green cloak, though in a lighter shade than the captain's.

He grabbed the paperwork out of Wiggin's hands and began to jot down the data needed, a sneer on his lips.

"What's more," the captain now almost shouted, "we are always appalled at the backwards-ness of this planet and its outdated and antiquated port landing systems. If Juno wasn't a hub for trading, we would have gone right through to Farth."

"Right!" the first mate chimed in, still scribbling answers on the declaration papers.

"Imagine," the captain said, "we have to fill out a paper form here just to let a squad of your longshoremen unload our cargo–by hand!" He busied himself by taking off his gloves and revealed soft and supple hands that had rings on almost every finger.

Wiggins cleared his throat before the first mate could chime in.

"Understood, Captain. Your comments–such as they are–will be relayed to the World Council when they meet next. 'Til then, I'm afraid that you must, yes, fill in these forms by hand. May I see the Customs and Health receipts please?" Wiggins held out his hand, awaiting the paperwork from Customs and Health that would certify the cargo and indicate any and all duties or taxes or even quarantines that would have to be paid or followed.

The Leudie captain glared at Wiggins, his hand stroking at his neck.

"And who, exactly, might you be? Some junior junior clerk whose only real job here is to feed your ugly balled-up Carnelian lizard?" he said as he snorted and petted the coiled rope of muscle that surrounded his neck.

Wiggins thought that the coil twitched for a moment, but knew that a Leudie neck snake would never uncoil unless it was hungry. Each Leudie had one of these "pets," given to them at puberty, and the two of them formed a pair bond that was unbreakable. It was said that the creature live its entire life wrapped around its owner's neck.

"I am the Assistant Assistant Port Keeper, Captain," Wiggins replied.

"Ah, yes! You're the little clerk who claimed we were exporting food items and wanted us to pay taxes on our passengers!" The captain smiled down at Wiggins and pointed a multi-ringed finger directly into his face.

"But when we appealed, your boss and even Rim Customs agreed with us, didn't they, little Assistant Assistant Port Keeper? They knew what we were doing was well within the legal limits. Too bad that was beyond you. Could have saved you much embarrassment, eh?" the captain gloated, his voice now soft and cloying as he shook his finger in Wiggins face.

Wiggins shuffled the papers in front of him, riding tight rein on his embarrassment.

"I mean, after all," he thought, "If you buy seafood, even live seafood from a fish distributor here on Juno, and then try to weasel out of paying your fair share of taxes by using the excuse that you were just transporting passengers to DenKoss, a water world 16 light-years away, anybody should have seen through that. The fact that the buyers on DenKoss had sworn that they were just trying to liberate some of their like species hadn't held water at all. Yet the Leudies had been able to force through their exemption, and the fees that Wiggins had originally charged had been negated. Score one for the Leudies.

"That's right, you were the Assistant Assistant who tried to penalize us for that little stopover to pick up passengers here. That was most unfair," said the captain.

"And whatever happened to your passengers, Captain? As I heard it, they wound up serving as dinner for DenKoss royalty," said Wiggins, losing the mental battle to keep the old frustrations suppressed.

"We had nothing at all to do with that. We didn't know, of course, so we're not to blame, right little clerk?" The captain leaned down on the counter. His face had turned a light gray, which for a blue-skinned Leudie meant that he found something funny. He stomped his foot, the boot heel smacking the wooden floor with a loud bang.

"Well, little clerk, what do you have to say about that mistake in judgment?" he said, as he roared.

"Actually, Captain, you know yourself that, while you can touch down on any of the planets out here on the Rim, if you off-load or on-load anything, you may be taxed on those items. And I was only following our laws here when I taxed you on the on-loaded seafood that you took to DenKoss. And as it sounds, I was right, wasn't I?" Wiggins looked directly at the Leudie, whose finger was still pointed at his face, and the captain's laughter subsiding.

"Not in the slightest, little clerk. We move things around, and we don't care what they are as long as there is a profit attached. It's bureaucrats like you who do the worrying. And on this trip, we're again looking to add to our cargo, so no more mistakes, little clerk!" He smiled down at Wiggins again and gathered up his gloves.

His first mate slid the paperwork over and in front of Wiggins before tugging at the hem of his captain's cloak. "Let's go, Captain. This one's too unimportant to even gloat over." He opened the door to leave the office.

"Far too unimportant. Most likely, as I figured, he's just the lizard's caregiver—and as ugly as his charge as well," the captain said as he stroked his neck snake and twirled the cloak around himself as he tromped down the stairs and walked back out onto the tarmac while Wiggins fumed.

He fussed with their paperwork and thought that, while he was over there at customs, he'd take a moment to look up Carnelian lizards and find out why they reacted so negatively to Leudies.

"So what'd you say then?" Allison asked. "Like, did you spit in his face or what? I mean he called you incompetent, almost, and he even said that those 'passengers' had been food all along. Boy, I'da grabbed–"

"I did nothing, Allison. I'm the Assistant Assistant Port Keeper, not the big cheese myself. Besides, there were two of them, and they were both big, even for Leudies, let me tell you," Wiggins said as he sat himself down opposite the port laundry clerk.

Allison had appeared one day about two years ago off an outward bound liner, had asked for the job of a laundry clerk, and had risen through hard work to now head her shift over at Port Laundry Services. She didn't sit with her crew anymore over on the far side of the Port Pub, as any good manager wouldn't do that. Instead, she had just one day sat down at the table occupied by most of the higher level assistant managers, and Wiggins, for one, thought she'd earned her place.

"Besides, the boss *and* Rim Customs agreed with their appeal, hence my own assessments were tossed," he said. But the fact that he'd remembered it and harbored a grudge was proof enough for Allison. Wiggins was still bothered by the incident.

Allison nodded. Her white uniform shirt was stained with blue laundry soap, but her smile was bright as sunshine as she stared down the wall to the table of Leudies sitting and drinking Juno Ale.

"Yeah, but I'da still popped him one. Got it coming; they all do. Did I ever tell you about my Aunt Estelle back inward on Tibettia in the Hosang system? She was a real tough cookie. She could call a man out and take a strip off him like nothing. Once, when a stranger..."

As Allison tried to regale him with another story about a relative, Wiggins let his attention wander and glanced around the room. The military crew of a Duchy ship, in their sparkling white uniforms, with all that pyrite braid and those chest-map ribbons, sat in the corner at long tables. They usually drank away from the port, but as Wiggins knew, they were just finishing up a quick one before they lifted off in the afternoon.

As they left, in came three Pentyaans and a couple of Quarans from Farth, a small planet just twenty light years away. Wiggins recognized only the Pentyaans as having been in the port before, but he knew that the Quarans would soon make his acquaintance in the port office one day. He watched as they got into the food line and loaded up their trays and a few moments later when they made their way to an empty table near the middle of the low-ceilinged room.

As usual, the Pentyaans sat on one side of the table, and the Quarans sat on the other,

"Even here, where we are all the same, awaiting loading and unloading, we tend to stick together," Wiggins thought.

Just beside them was a table full of Marines from Conclusion, another human home world out here on the Rim. Wiggins watched them as they paid no mind to anyone or anything. They wolfed down their heavily laden trays and washed it all down with ale.

"Like most soldiers, you can bet they know that you never turn down good food and ale, but I bet they know how to listen to a story." Allison dropped her comment in nicely to chide Wiggins and his wandering attention.

"Sorry, Allison, but I noticed the Duchy crew moving out, and then in came those Pentyaans. And...I'm sorry. You were saying?" Wiggins smiled at her, hoping she wasn't angry.

"Well, you missed my point is all. What I was trying to tell you is that there is always another way to skin a cat that you just maybe haven't thought of as yet. I know you a little, Wiggins, and I know that now you know that the recently arrived Leudie captain fooled everyone into letting him get away with no taxes last time—that you're now thinking about how to get even with that big galoot because you were right all along. Am I right here or what?" She looked directly at Wiggins, her eyes piercing his.

He looked at her and was about to nod and then stopped himself. "Not even close, Allison. That was in the past, and I'm beyond trying to get revenge on a trader. But you are correct in that it does seem that I was right, and they did avoid paying tax via a subterfuge that only I, it seems, was willing to question. However, life goes on, even out here on the Rim," he said, his voice firm as he stared right back at Allison.

"Bullfeathers, Wiggins. I know you...but anyways, you did miss the story of my Aunt Estelle, and I'll have to remember to tell it to you some other time." She finished up her large glass of what passed on Juno for a fruit juice and slurped the dregs at the bottom of the glass.

With a jab of her straw she stabbed the cherry at the bottom of the plas glass and slid it off and into her mouth. She sucked on it for a moment, studying Wiggins and then shrugged as she chewed and swallowed.

"So, you going back right now, or have you got something else up?" she asked as she stood by their table near the wall, straightening her uniform and gathering up her tray to bus her own table.

"I have to go back and crank out some paperwork. Spent an hour earlier this morning over at customs looking up Jinni's background. You know that she always shrinks and tries to hide every time a Leudie comes into the port offices, right? You want to know why?" he asked.

She grunted and motioned with her straws.

"Sure she can't keep them out, are you?" she said wishfully.

He shook his head.

"No, sorry. Fact is, Carnelian lizards are very susceptible to ty radiation, not a generally known fact. And another little known fact, Leudie neck snakes exude the stuff. It's their damn snakes that make Jinni feel so bad she tries to go into hibernation. So even my pet doesn't like them." he said.

"Let's walk back together," Wiggins said as he rose and carried his own dishes over to the server's station near the entrance. After passing the table with the Leudies, he held the door open for Allison, and as he turned to walk out the door behind Allison, he thought he could hear the table burst into laughter at something their captain had said.

"This has gotta' stop," he thought. He felt his ears redden as he double-stepped down the front stairs and hit the pavement below. Soon, real soon...

Once back at the office, Wiggins began to assault the stack of paperwork that was the bane of his existence. He checked and re-checked each cargo manifest to make sure it matched the customs declaration filled in by the visitors, and then he checked it all again by hand with each entry made by the customs officials who inspected each and every hold on every ship that landed here. Then there was the background data on each cargo item that he had to check on—what it was, what it was to be used for, where it was going, and any and all hazardous materials notices—cautions due to proximity or improper storage, affects of gravity or radiation or vacuum on the cargo itself, etc.

When all of that tallied true, he then checked each cargo allotment against the exempt listings, and when an item was not tax exempt, he assessed the taxes due and put those numbers in the right columns again for each and every ship that had both landed and taken off that day. Then, he double-checked all of the cargo listings that captains had tendered to the office for sale and updated the postings for all to see. That way, each captain who had cargo to sell or wanted to take on more could check on the one listing and buy or sell directly based on that list.

Once that was done, he then tallied all of the taxes owed by each ship and posted the same with his financial office as well as with the customs computers, and then finally, he walked the finished paperwork out to each ship to hand-deliver the latest assessments to each ship's captain.

Most were fine with what they owed as they'd already computed the same before even taking on the cargo. Even the Leudies knew ahead of time what to expect for the most part—their tricks notwithstanding.

Wiggins also had to man the counter in the office and was working on his accounts when he heard the slow trudge of feet on the steps outside the office front door. Each step sounded like it was a chore, and the door opened slowly.

Ttseens, Wiggins thought, and he was right. Ttseens were often referred to as dog people. They looked mostly like a cross between a short human and a boxer dog, muzzle and all. Ttseens had whiskers like boxers and the same pointed ears that stuck out at the top of their heads. Down their back, a stub of a tail could often be seen wagging when they were happy, which was most of the time.

Late to come to FTL, they had only been around for about a century or so as a part of the Rim culture, and as such, they needed to import just about everything. They considered themselves traders, but Wiggins knew that they weren't in the Leudie's league. He put on his clerk's smile and got the paperwork ready for them as they came in.

"Morning there, Port Keeper. Got some paperwork for you," the larger of the two said to Wiggins, and he dropped a sheaf of papers on the counter. He looked over at the office pet and said, "Stay away, Junior," to his companion, who was already inching along the counter towards the end where the caged lizard lay.

Jinni had un-balled herself but was still backed into the corner, her wings jammed tight on her shoulders as her back sail drooped over to one side.

"Thanks—Captain, is it?" Wiggins said as he turned the paperwork around to read it and began to study the checklist on the top.

"Captain Smullick, here, and my son, Junior, who's our first mate," he said.

Wiggins watched his whiskers bounce with every word. At about 80% the height of a human but only 50% of their weight, the Ttseens were a thin race who often wore layer after layer of clothing. Wiggins had heard that someone had tried to get them interested in lightweight but fully insulated clothing a while back, but that this had never sold well with them.

Their planet, also called Ttseen, was only 5000km in diameter, which meant that it had only about 60% of the gravity here, which made Ttseens seem very weak and slow. But Wiggins knew they were as sharp mentally as anyone else who landed here, except maybe for Leudies.

Wiggins nodded to the captain. "Nice to meet you, Captain, and you too, Junior." He turned to see the youngster edging a fingertip between the bars of the cage. "Whoops, you don't want to do that. Jinni is quite a hermit, and if she wanted to, she'd nip off that finger."

The boy pulled his finger back slowly. He looked over at Wiggins as Jinni yawned and showed off her teeth—an impressive set for sure.

"Gee, thanks. I've never seen such a pet before. But I won't let her bite me."

"His big brown eyes add to the 'looks-like-a-boxer-dog' theory," thought Wiggins, glad that he'd been able to look up the long extinct dog breed over at customs in the *Encyclopedia Galactica* a while back. "Wonder if they'd fetch a stick," he thought before turning back to the paperwork and quashing a small smirk that appeared for a moment on his face.

"Everything seems in order," he said. "However, I see that you've got a whole load of diamonds from Eons. Customs says they're chemical diamonds and not natural ones?" Wiggins asked, as there could be a tax issue there.

Natural diamonds were always exempt if already part of a ship's cargo, but these were brand new diamonds he'd never heard about before, and if they were grown in chemical farms, they might be taxable.

"That's right, Port Keeper, they are the latest and newest form of diamonds, chemically grown, it is true. The cults on Eons have mastered the art of growing diamonds, and we grabbed the first cargo allowed off planet. And as noted, while these are industrial grade diamonds, we feel they should be treated the same as natural diamonds and therefore be tax exempt."

The captain's whiskers still bounced for a couple of seconds after he had finished speaking, but his eyes never left Wiggins.

"He believes he's correct," Wiggins thought. He asked the question that would determine all.

"And what is the chemical nature of the base material, Captain?"

"Thorium, the paperwork says. Atomic Number 90. And they used Isotope 7, which is much longer lived when it comes to water solubility. It makes them the perfect item for drill bits and industrial grinders, both of which use pressurized streams of water for their lubrication. We're happy we grabbed that first shipment, and we will look for a buyer here on Juno starting later today."

"Any problems with them at all, Captain, usage wise?" Wiggins asked.

"Not a one, Port Keeper. They are at least 75% cheaper than naturals and supposedly they'll last 50% longer," he said with a chuckle as he crossed his arms in front of his small chest and stuck his muzzle straight out.

"Made his point, he believes," Wiggins thought and nodded to the captain.

"Fine, Captain, however I will have to do the reading on those diamonds myself, just to assure customs that they pose no problems now or in the future. So you're tax free on this landing—so far, mind you. Take on any more cargo or sell and off-load anything, and things could change. I'll put a three hour hold on the diamonds 'til I've read the specs, which should be enough. I'll notify you when we release them. Anti-matter fill, too?

"Right, Port Keeper. Once that hold is lifted, we'll be out to sell the diamonds, at a good profit, too, we figure. Thank you, Port Keeper, and 'til later. Junior?" the captain said.

His son made his own goodbyes, and they both moved slowly out of the office and across the tarmac towards their landing pad.

Wiggins turned towards the stack of hard copy files and realized he'd better get started. He read and read and read, and just about at the end, he stopped at something he saw printed before him in a tiny list of cautions. He looked up and out the window of the Port Keeper's office, his eyebrows pulled down low.

Outside and somewhat away from the office, he could see the ships standing on their pads, most still with cargo bay ramps up, and the scurrying of the port's longshoremen. He shook his head.

"Wait," he thought, and he looked down again at that list to read it carefully, to soak up every word and understand exactly what the cautions on these new diamonds might mean.

He read.

And then he thought again.

And then he smiled.

Later, in the Port Pub, at the end of the business day, Wiggins wormed his way across the crowded noisy floor to the manager's table that was almost full. Squeezing onto the end of the bench, he faced Allison and grinned at her broadly.

"So, your work's done for the day, I expect, judging from that ale in front of you," he said as he caught the barmaid's eye and signaled for two of the same.

"Sure is, Wiggins," she said as she leaned forward so she didn't have to yell over the hubbub of the Pub and its drinkers. Around them, all the tables were almost full. They were three deep at the bar and mostly filling the aisles as well. There was another whole squad of Marines who were playing some drinking game. Beside them and egging them on were Duchy navy men, their white dress uniforms no longer so pristine.

"And you? Had a good day did you, judging by that smile?" she added, as she lifted her fresh glass to toast him. He did the same, and after the glasses clinked, he swallowed heartily.

"I did. I had a very good day. In fact, you could say, I fulfilled the duties of the Assistant Assistant Port Keeper to the fullest," he smiled at her again and had to lean in as three Quarans passed by, walking shoulder-to-shoulder and all singing loudly as they searched for a table, all six arms entwined.

"And how's that, exactly?" she asked. "Your day didn't start out too well with those Leudies," she said as she scowled and shook her head. "I would'a popped him one, myself." She swiped her mouth with the sleeve of her laundry uniform.

He nodded to her, and his smile never wavered.

"Assistant Assistant Port Keepers do not 'pop' anyone, Allison. Our job is to take care of all landing details for anyone who touches down here on Juno. And, if possible, we also pass along cargo requests and offers, which is what I did just a half-hour ago. And to the same Leudie crew, too."

She choked on the swallow that was halfway down her throat and coughed back a mouthful into her glass. "You what? Your brain turn to mush, Wiggins? You helped those traders?" she said.

He nodded, and the smile got broader.

"Fact is, I knew that they were going to Farth, a twenty day trip with mining equipment already in their hold. And I knew that they were looking for more cargo to take all the way there or drop off in-between. And I also knew that a small ship had come from Eons with a cargo that was for sale and that it would be perfect for use on Farth—new industrial diamonds for their drilling equipment. All I did was link the two of them together, and they made a deal."

"New diamonds?" she asked.

"Special ones, chemically grown and at least 50% less costly than natural diamonds. And I knew that the Leudies would figure that into their deal and would pay more here to make a killing on the other end. These diamonds are a perfect item for the mining that goes on over on Farth," he said as he finished his ale and looked for the barmaid to get a couple more drinks brought over to the table.

"Are you nuts, Wiggins?" she barked at him, shaking her head.

"Ahh, well first, of course, I had to ensure that these new diamonds were safe. So I had to read more than sixty pages of tiny printed disclaimers. And it seems they'll do the job alright. They will make perfect raw materials for application as drill bit diamonds. Except..." he paused as the new ales arrived, and he took a swig.

Allison didn't pick up her fresh one and stared at him, her fingers gesturing to urge him on.

"Except what, Wiggins?" she asked.

"Well, they can turn into mush, totally unusable, should they be anywhere near one certain kind of radiation over a period of at least ten days," he said as he drank long from the glass.

Allison grinned, and then she too drank and wiped her mouth with her sleeve.

"Ah, the Leudie neck snake kind, I suspect," and she held up her glass for a cheers.

Wiggins grinned from ear to ear as the two glasses clinked and ordered two more right away. Ω

A Thin Atmosphere, Chapter 1

Written By
Dan Colton

Lieutenant Commander Derry Genny wasn't a complainer. He made sure of it.

"You can't bitch and moan all day long and sit in my seat," he liked to lecture his wife and son.

Sasha, Genny's wife, generally smiled politely back at him. In a rare sour mood, she'd roll her eyes and clank her fork loudly on her plate.

Genny was worried about Reggie, his son. He couldn't tell what the boy was thinking. Genny was a star in the Coalition Navy, the most veteran and celebrated lieutenant commander in the fighter corps, hero of the Jupiter Station pirate wars, and though he would never admit it, his son made him more nervous than any mission he'd ever flown. Reggie was only seventeen, but his eyes were older. Genny didn't understand the boy.

The father and son weren't much alike outside of physical appearance. Both were tall and well-shouldered with short cropped hair they never let grow too long, wide eyes, and serious faces. But not much else between them was held in common.

Often, when Genny rambled on about one harrowing adventure or another, as he was prone to do, he'd look over to see his son buried nose-deep in the screen of a digitext. The boy seemed more interested in the pages of his histories than the adrenaline-pumping tales his father could recall first-hand.

Genny told himself there was more of Sasha in the boy, a quirk both of genetics and of familiarity. Genny had been a young recruit in the Coalition Navy when Reggie had been born. He had spent much of the boy's childhood flying sorties above the front lines. Reggie's quiet nature was distinctly Sasha.

"Reggie, are you listening?" said Genny.

"Yeah, Dad," said Reggie quietly, looking up from his lap. His dinner was untouched.

"I was just saying how complainers don't get very far in life," said Genny.

"Alright," said Reggie, "I know. I don't complain."

"I'm not saying you do, son. I just wish—"

The phone rang. Sasha stood. At thirty-five, she was still just as beautiful as the day eighteen years before when Genny had married her shortly before boarding the transport to basic. They'd finally found the time to celebrate their eighteenth anniversary three weeks earlier.

The phone rang again. "I'll get it," said Sasha.

She placed her thumb onto the activation switch of the small phone. It read her thumbprint and connected the call's transmission wirelessly to a tiny device behind her ear.

"Hello?" said Sasha.

She alone heard the response, "Ma'am, I need to speak with Lieutenant Commander Genny immediately, please."

"One moment," said Sasha. She knew that tone and what it meant.

"Derry," said Sasha. "It's for you." She deftly tossed him the small receiver, and he activated it with his thumb.

"Hello?" said Derry. "This is Genny."

"We've got a problem."

Genny didn't have any issue getting through the cordoned-off checkpoints. His conversation with the man on the phone, a Major Bradley Anthon, had ended dinner early. He hadn't bothered to change his clothes. His old, black denim jeans, a white, thermo-woven t-shirt, and his reliable brown poly-fiber boots would be fine for now. He had also strapped on his old wristwatch, which still ticked dependably even during the era of digital everything.

He checked the time. It was 5:43 in the evening.

Soon, it wouldn't matter what he'd worn. He'd be in his flight suit.

There hadn't been much explanation on the phone, but Genny hadn't asked a lot of questions. Another rocket attack from the Rebels had struck the Coalition's sensor generator. Their orbital tracking systems were now effectively blind.

Because no other options to monitor air security existed, all available pilots were being scrambled to manually monitor radar activity in the air, and that meant that Genny and the three other pilots in his squad would spend the next several days in the air as frequently as not. Each craft would act independently as a remote radar device with a crew of one pilot and one technician. As one squad reached the end of its patrol shift, another would be in route to take its place.

Leaving his apartment, Genny stepped into the metallic corridor leading from his chambers. The airtight windows along the white, sterile hallway showed a beautiful landscape of lush ferns and tall rainforest canopies outside. They were a convincing illusion—holograms. Mars was hardly the place for a scenic view. Engineers had installed the projectors to combat claustrophobia.

Genny rather liked the rainforest setting and the occasional glimpse of a tiger retreating into the trees as if you were actually intruding on its privacy. Of course, Genny had never seen a real tiger. Earth—where, he'd been told, tigers had once lived—was just a bright light in the distance. Centuries of mechanized terraforming had returned Earth to near pristine condition, and efforts to recolonize were underway. The bright planet on the horizon was a mystery, filled with forgotten pasts and raw materials to harvest and bring elsewhere.

Mars was not a place you could describe as beautiful. Stark, maybe. Unforgiving, definitely. With many a mission flown above this desolate crag of a planet, Derry Genny knew all too well the realities of the murderous environment.

Once, fifteen years prior, Genny had been ordered to fly a reconnaissance route over a swath of the Rebel-held Martian wastes. The land was flat and nearly featureless. The Rebels—anarchists and religious zealots—were apt engineers who built pressurized, subterranean tunnel systems. Some of the stronger Rebel factions sometimes had the wherewithal to erect surface-to-air missile systems, which directly jeopardized the Coalition's air security.

Halfway through that fated recon patrol, a rogue missile fired from the lifeless expanse below had locked onto the heat signature of Genny's ship. Initial avoidance maneuvers failed to shake the tracer, and forced to eject, Genny had spent three days camped inside an emergency chamber-tent.

His wife, busy with their infant child, had been informed that her husband had been shot down over the Martian frontier. For three days, Sasha had feared him dead while Genny had waited for rescue—terrified, hungry, and alone. Blaster in hand, he had sleeplessly waited for a Rebel attack that never came. After he was lifted to rescue, a nuclear warhead had decimated the missile site, but that fact had brought Genny no solace. The Rebels were notoriously expert diggers and had likely been safe below the Martian crust.

Now, fifteen years later, Rebel advances had grown bolder and closer to the colony's doorstep. Rockets fired from the surrounding canyons reached even into Mars City Starport. Coalition seismologists monitoring Rebel excavation activities along the border were often killed or held hostage. Observation posts were going dark. Threats were slipping through the wire and compromising vital security systems.

Genny caught the X-Train headed from his apartment bloc towards the starport. A crowd of six or seven people attempted to board the X-Train, but stun-bat wielding officers denied them.

Genny flashed his military ID and was allowed through to the jeers of the annoyed commuters. It was 6:15 P.M. as the X-Train's door slid shut.

The shabby and windowless transit shuttle was entirely abandoned aside from Derry and a uniformed guard reservist with a pile of bags around his feet. The reservist seemed impatient, afraid, or both. Chevrons on his shoulders marked him as a private.

News bulletins displayed throughout the shuttle declared a state of emergency across the entire colony: "Military mobilizes emergency deployment in response to Rebel rocket attacks. All non-essential personnel, remain in your dwellings. Do not interfere."

The shuttle vibrated across its magnetic track almost silently. Errant static electricity cracked and buzzed from the friction of the shuttle's antigravity propulsion. Travelling at over 300 miles per hour, the shuttle made quick time out of the colony's sprawl. The news bulletin switched automatically to the more familiar: "Now leaving Mars City. Population 2,747,043 and growing!"

The screen switched again, almost immediately: "Now Entering Mars Starport. ATTN: Security measures have been elevated. Please have ID available immediately for inspection."

Genny was reading but not paying much attention to the bulletins. Just like the reservist, Genny was impatient. As the train slowed to a stop, the commander's fellow passenger walked towards the shuttle exit, luggage strapped around his shoulder, ID ready for inspection.

The train continued on for another five minutes until an abrupt halt shook its titanium frame. The fluorescent lights flickered briefly. The two men waited.

The hiss of pressurization surrounded the windowless shuttle, and soon, the exit door slid open. Five smartly-dressed Coalition guardsmen boarded and inspected the two men's identification. The trip extended for another brief moment down track, and the shuttle bypassed several civilian drop-off points. It headed directly for the Coalition Air Force hangar and launch strip. As the hangar area grew closer, the Coalition guardsmen seemed to become anxious. The elite troops remained silent. Genny waited for the transit to be over.

His wristwatch read 6:54 P.M. when the Coalition guardsmen handed the two passengers pressure masks and opened the shuttle door to the Martian air. The night was especially dark this far from the main settlement, and the air pressure escaping from the shuttle caused the sand outside to blow and swirl.

Explosions could be heard in the distance.

Within six minutes, Genny was inside the flight control room for a briefing. The mood among the pilots and their technicians was tense and alert, if a bit reserved.

With the threat of Rebel missile attack a distinct possibility, piloted radar-patrol craft needed to immediately establish a complete sensor sweep of every inch of Coalition airspace.

The haste and nervousness with which the briefing officer spoke left Genny slightly dismayed, and he brought it up with his onboard technician, Iso Wanatabe—Tabe to those who knew him well.

"Seems to me something's got everyone spooked around here," Genny said to his technician and zipped up his black flight suit. "You heard anything as to why?"

"Only the standard stuff about the Rebel rocket attack. Beyond that, nothing," Wanatabe said. "Something else must be happening, I agree. I heard some explosions when I got off the Tram. Did you?"

Genny didn't answer. His attention had already switched to the mission. They left the briefing room and moved toward the hangar together. The hangar floor was abuzz with activity. Pilots and technicians ran last-minute diagnostics while the fighter craft were lined up. Ordinance handlers loaded canisters of charge into the weapons batteries.

Wanatabe was a short man—available space onboard the Zephyte X2X Worshipper spacecraft was slim. The lion's share of leftover room was usually reserved for the pilot. With the addition of radar equipment, a secondary man was absolutely necessary to operate all systems outside of navigation.

Genny couldn't be happier to have the adept, young technician at his back. If things got hairy, Tabe could also take the role of turret gunner. Though he was untested in battle—

almost all of the Coalition's enlisted men were these days—Genny had watched the recruit during fire and maneuver drills. After seeing Tabe in action, Genny had requested that the talented young man fly with him during any duo missions.

Genny and Wanatabe took their seats in the lead ship and waited for the other crews to fall in behind.

As the Worshipper spacejet taxied onto the launch pad for vertical takeoff, Wanatabe and Genny saw why everyone on base was so on edge. Less than a mile away, across the flat Martian plain, bursts of automatic laser fire danced to and fro. Blue-electric ion cannons hummed and erupted with jets of pulse beams while aircraft dodged anti-air lasers and relentlessly bombed the enemy artillery. The darkness of the Martian night was interrupted by vibrant action from the hundreds of deadly projectiles.

The briefing officer had failed to mention—perhaps had been too frightened or distracted to mention—that the entire spaceport was under heavy perimeter assault by a large and aggressive Rebel force.

As Genny and Wanatabe moved slowly into launching position, they saw dozens of reservists load up into land cruisers and drive off along rough roads in the direction of the battle.

Wanatabe's voice came through faintly across an encrypted channel, though he was seated just two feet behind Genny. "I've never seen anything like it..."

"Don't focus on that. Focus on our mission. Radar is down, and a barrage of Rebel missiles could get through at any moment. These are nukes we're talking about." Genny checked his watch. It was just past 7:24 P.M. "We've got to get eyes in the sky."

Both men were busy running final diagnostics and bringing dormant systems to life. The dual jet and ion engines allowed the craft to maneuver both inside and outside of an atmosphere. The mission that day required an altitude of eleven kilometers, keeping them just inside the thin atmosphere's roof. Besides the attached radar equipment, almost all Coalition craft were uniformly equipped with heat-sensing warning systems which could detect the friction of a missile penetrating through an atmosphere, among other things. Occasionally, meteorites passing through an atmosphere's barrier would fool a pilot into reporting a missile detection, and many of the old hands ignored the small heat-signature panel almost completely. But today, Genny's eyes constantly flicked down to the small display.

They were given the order to take off, and by the time they were at 25,000 feet, the cloudless, dark sky around the craft was rife with wing lights. Anti-air fire flew into the air a mile off of the squad's eastern wingtips. More Coalition craft joined the circular formation, and the grouping gained altitude as it grew. Radio chatter was nonstop.

Genny again checked the pressurization and weaponry readouts. Everything was running optimally. He was about to relax back into the seat when Wanatabe's voice shot over the intercom.

"Incoming surface missile fire."

Outside of drills, it was the first time he'd spoken such words.

Genny overheard other technicians on the radio shout out similar warnings as an onboard alarm gave him further alert of the explosive ordinance. Pure piloting instinct kicked in, and Genny swung the ship into a steep climb. He turned like a spinning top and released flares to confuse any heat-seeking missiles.

As the plane ascended, inertia plunged the two men backwards into their seats. The ship's frame protested against the strain.

Genny took a harried moment to look out through the cockpit window towards the surface of Mars. White exhaust twisted from dozens and dozens Rebel rockets, nipping at the tail ends of the lower-altitude fighters. A few squadrons had yet to reach 30,000 feet. Too low to escape, the lower-altitude Coalition craft were clipped by the missiles and exploded.

"My gods..." Wanatabe moaned.

As Genny and Wanatabe continued to climb to safety higher and higher out of the atmosphere, the only noise was of the ship's hull being battered by speed. The radio was alive with cries of distress.

A blindingly bright flash of light filled the cockpit. For a moment, all electrical systems ceased functioning. The control panel went dead, and the plane slipped into a stall. Darkness and the sound of open air surrounded Tabe and Genny.

A second later, the systems came back on, and Genny breathlessly pulled the ship out of the dive and continued to climb.

Wanatabe looked back at the surface for the first time and saw a growing mushroom cloud five miles below.

Tabe cried out, "Damn it, the colony! They've nuked the colony!"

Genny engaged jet thrusters and twisted up as the mushroom cloud gained slack behind them.

There was a long moment of silence. Neither of the two men could speak. They just kept looking over their shoulders to see the ominous cloud rise from the darkness down below.

The other craft in the attachment had fallen out of contact in the frantic scramble to escape the missile barrage. Comm links were lost. If the air armada still functioned as a force, Genny and Tabe were in the wrong place. They weren't picking up any radio chatter.

The missile-lock warning shrieked.

"MISSILE. MISSILE," shouted Wanatabe.

Genny's twitch reflexes were all that saved them. He adjusted the craft's pitch just in time to dodge the deadly projectile. Both men watched while the fifteen-foot white rocket streaked by just below the plane's nose. The missile began a sharp turn back, but Genny released a trio of flares. The missile dropped away with the decoys. It contacted a flare and exploded nearly too close. Light shrapnel peppered the ship's titanium frame.

Still another great explosion rumbled beneath them.

"What's happening?" Wanatabe, breathless and trembling, asked.

Genny didn't reply immediately. He checked pressurization and weaponry readouts once more. All still seemed perfectly functional. Fuel levels could last for twelve hours of jet engine flight, and his outer-drive engine was ready for two days of nonstop spaceflight. But comm links were dead.

"Looks like we're alone out here. No communications," Genny said.

A wave of turbulence from the nuclear strike reverberated through the craft. Even the powerful onboard voice communication system—supposedly EMP proof—threw static.

Wanatabe wasn't holding together nearly as well as his pilot. "What are we going to do?" the younger man said, seemingly pleading with Genny for reassurance.

"First off, we abandon the plan," said Genny. Debris from the rocket attack against the Zephytes still fell towards the ground as the mushroom clouds continued to push upward. "The airspace is compromised. We're leaving the atmosphere. Prepare to enter outer space."

Genny checked his watch out of habit. The entire takeoff, engagement, and disengagement into space had lasted exactly thirteen minutes. It was 7:37 P.M. as they exited the thin atmosphere of Mars and crossed over the brim of space.

Once in orbit, they were safe. Wary of Rebels who might've hijacked the Coalition's suborbital defenses, Genny disengaged the engine along with all other nonessential systems.

"Current bearing?" asked Genny over the onboard intercom for the fifth time in two minutes.

On the edge of the atmosphere, tensions were high. The risk of atmospheric friction made the likelihood of being discovered increase tenfold.

"Maintaining a constant bearing, sir," the technician reported. "Nothing's changed. Believe me," he said, "I'm keeping an eye on it."

It had only been twenty minutes since gaining orbit, but it already felt like days. Both men sat quietly and waited for outside word to come across their Zephyte Worshipper's communications system.

At a few seconds after 10:15 P.M., they picked up a faint transmission from the Martian surface.

"...ed systems..." the channel refused to hold a steady broadcast, "...rn to base to regroup...overrun and pulling..."

"Do you hear that?" Wanatabe cheered. "They're still alive down there! Did you hear that?"

"Calm down," growled Genny. His already tired nerves had frayed even further as they had waited for word from the ground. "We don't know anything about the situation."

"What do you mean? We've received contact! It's what we've been waiting for, sir!"

"Nothing is safe until we establish steady confirmation. We don't know who is talking to us down there." Genny made a vain attempt to orient the incoming signal with more focused power and then brought the Worshipper's jet engines back online. "The nuclear clouds must be hampering comm signals. Wanatabe, prepare to drop out of orbit," Genny ordered.

"Aye, aye," replied Wanatabe.

Genny angled the silver Zephyte towards the surface of Mars. It was just after 10:17 P.M. "Wanatabe, prepare the surveillance camera."

"Yes, sir," said the technician. "What do you think you'll see?"

"There's only one thing I can say for sure. The colony is a big place, hundreds of miles wide. No single nuke in existence today is capable of a blast radius larger than thirty miles.

And complete damage from a bomb would only occur within a five-mile radius of the hypocenter, at most. No, even three nukes couldn't wipe out all of the colony's life-support functions. People are still alive down there. There's no doubt about that."

"Then it's a matter of who survived and if they want us there," Wanatabe said.

He was right. Although the past hours had been a blur, Genny still vividly recalled the image of the three mushroom clouds during their flight out of the atmosphere. The assault had been a complete surprise, and the entire colony could be overrun. The men had no way to know for sure.

"Don't focus on that," said Genny. "When I take over on the cameras, you'll have to man flight controls. I need the ship steady. Keep a straight pitch and throttle constant so I can focus the pictures. We need them. Got it?" said Genny.

"Got it."

A moment later, Genny dropped the Zephyte into a low orbit above Mars. Even in the dark of midnight, evidence of the nuclear strikes was still painful and evident—smoke, red and ionized, billowed up from the nuclear blast sites, the superheated plumes still electrically-charged and radioactive. The clouds hung over the region and met at the top of the atmosphere, as if a single, supernatural blaze had ravaged an unfortunate swath of the planet.

"Can't see anything from here. Got to get below that smoke ceiling," said Genny.

"Yes, sir," said Wanatabe. "Dropping below the cloud layer." He banked the Zephyte gently to the left, away from the ionic danger. The horizon swung.

"Depress pitch to bearing one-four-three. Increase speed to 350."

Wanatabe evened out the swing and sped up. As they crossed around the cloud's edge, Genny took detailed pictures in rapid succession. The two other ion clouds were faint in the background, and almost no bare ground was discernable through the smoke. The hull-mounted camera swiveled and recorded it all feverishly.

"Adjust to bearing one-eight-zero," said Genny.

As they continued the flight above the expansive colony complex below, Genny viewed it all through his infrared telescopic lens, taking the occasional snashot.

The starport appeared to have been leveled. The battleground was a waste of bodies, a defaced, laser-scarred land. Away from the starport, along the X-Tram lines, Genny could make out bands of Rebels moving across the landscape in rovers and in pressure suits, busy with derailment, demolition, and sabotage missions. The X-Tram had thousands upon thousands of miles of track, and Genny recognized a concerted, planned effort y the Rebels to disrupt the lines along strategic bottlenecks to make intra-colony transportation a near impossibility.

One word came to the Genny's mind: siege.

His final photo was of his own apartment complex, roughly 300 miles from the starport. Rebel activity seemed focused within a 100-mile perimeter of the port. Genny estimated that the central Rebel force at roughly 1,000 fighters based on the activity below. Beyond the 100-mile perimeter, however, he saw very little Rebel presence on the surface of Mars, though it would take weeks, if not months, to search every corner of the colony and find every last Rebel.

Genny did see several clusters of a dozen or so individuals standing behind improvised bulwarks in the open spaces between buildings. He hoped they were Coalition troops, but the infrared vision offered no finer details.

"Sir," said Wanatabe. "I've located the broadcast we heard it orbit. It's coming from an apartment bloc region. I've forwarded the location to your display."

Apartments on Mars were established in dense clusters at several locations throughout the colony. Genny felt a flood of hope when he realized the signal pulsed from his family's bloc.

"Good, Wanatabe. Establish a link."

"I've been trying, sir, but I've had no luck. There's so much radiation of every kind in the air right now, it's too hard for the comm waves to get through."

Genny waited a moment. Options were running thin. "I think we need to land and investigate the signal on foot," said Genny. "Are you up for it?"

"I have to be up for it," said Wanatabe. "We can't stay in this Zephyte forever."

Wanatabe changed course and headed for the communication signal in the apartment bloc. The unspoken problem both men understood had to do with landing the Worshipper. All Zephyte craft, including the Worshipper, took off and landed vertically and required no airstrip. Under normal circumstances, this was a huge tactical advantage, but the powerful thrusters exceeded temperatures of 3,100 degrees Fahrenheit. They would destroy all but the most resistant alloys. To land on bare Martian ground was unthinkable.

"We'll have to crash land on our belly," said Genny

"Alright, sir. I'm ready," said Tabe.

Genny decreased speed as much as possible. The heavy craft had no natural lift and would land hard, so the hull's sheer durability would be its only saving grace. Genny and Wanatabe braced for impact with a final approach speed of over 200 miles per hour. If Genny could bring them in at just the right angle, there was a good chance the Worshipper would hold together. The midnight Martian ground rose silently as the Zephyte descended. Both Genny and Tabe held on as best they could and watched the altitude meter steadily approach zero.

Immediately upon impact, the Zephyte began to drag its left wing against the ground, and the ship rebounded violently. It cascaded to a stop in a long, carved gnash.

Things went dark for Genny before impact. When he came to shortly afterwards, his vision was unfocused and painful like a hangover. A fire had broken out inside the oxygen-rich technician's cabin, and Tabe was trying to struggle out of his seat and away from the flames. Genny engaged the fire suppression system, cursing the computer for not engaging it automatically, but the damage was already done.

Genny silently reached back and, popping the access door to Tabe's cabin, injected adrenaline into his technician's thigh. Within a few heartbeats, Wanatabe's pain receded.

"Put on your pressure suit, if you can," said Genny. "We have to make it inside."

The sedatives brought Wanatabe's pain just within a bearable threshold. "Shit," he groaned. "It hurts, sir."

"We have to move," said Genny.

There was no sense wasting time. They climbed down out of the Zephyte two miles from the nearest apartment bloc. It was slow going, but they reached their destination with an hour of oxygen left. Wanatabe hadn't complained of pain and had managed to keep pace with Genny, but he desperately needed medical attention.

They walked around the wall of the apartment complex until they saw a small gate. They took up a spot below the terminal's sensors to await a response from inside. None came. Not even the computer interface at the terminal responded.

"There's no power coming through to the gate," said Genny after a moment's observation. He walked towards the pressure-lock door, and with a tentative motion, extended his hand and depressed the open button. It swung open to reveal the chamber inside.

"Power lock is down," said Genny, turning back to his technician. "Something's compromised it. It's hacked from the inside."

Wanatabe stumbled ahead and lost his footing.

"Just hang in there," Genny said, helping the wounded man up. "I'll try to find you something for the pain."

Genny led Wanatabe inside the inner chamber and shut the door to Mars. A dim, orange backup light slowly came on inside.

Wanatabe appeared dizzy and close to collapse. He leaned against the cold chamber wall to gain a spot of rest.

The two remained silent as the pressurization chamber equalized. During the interval, Genny reached into his survival pack and retrieved a small blaster pistol. Wanatabe followed his example, but he moved slowly, doubled-over and sick with pain.

As the pressurization cycle hissed to an end, both men removed their pressure masks and helmets. Genny, in front of Wanatabe, faced the door which led into the apartment complex, his blaster pistol raised and at the ready.

"Sir," said Wanatabe weakly from behind, "we don't know if the Rebels are on the other side of this door, do we?"

"No, Tabe. No, we don't." Genny moved right up beside the door and knelt. Wanatabe was next to him on the left with barely enough strength to raise his blaster.

"Muster up, Tabe. We have to go."

They moved into the apartment corridor. In the dim, orange backup light, the long hallway lacked its usual uniform, sterilized whiteness. Some of the apartment doors were open, and before Genny moved through into the hallway, he gave them all a hard look. He had no idea which buildings the Rebels currently occupied, how to find the exact location of the distress signal, or where to go to rejoin his family.

"Which way?" Tabe whispered. He needed to find aid.

The chamber light flickered one last time and fell dark, and only the pale, faint outline of the whitewashed walls remained visible.

"Straight," said Genny as his eyes adjusted. They moved toward the far end of the corridor where it took a sharp turn to the right.

Genny held up his hand as they neared a corner. Wanatabe waited nervously while Genny dared a furtive glance down the next hall.

Thirty meters down the dark corridor, two men stood outside of an open apartment door. Both were distracted by a commotion within the apartment. A fluorescent lamp inside the apartment spilled out into the darkened hallway. The outlines of the men's outdated blaster rifles were clear enough in the silver-white silhouette.

Genny turned to Wanatabe.
"Rebels," he whispered and felt his blood turn cold. Ω

Read the next exciting chapter of **A Thin Atmosphere** *in Issue 2 of*
Nonlocal Science Fiction!

Deal Gone Bad, Chapter 1

Written By
Thad Kanupp

I woke up with a scorpion on my face. It was crunchier than I prefer, but I've had worse breakfasts. I crawled out of the scrub patch where I'd slept, tongue poking at the chitin stuck in my teeth. Dew had beaded across my skin overnight, and I was shivering. By noon, I would trade it for sweat under the ruthless wasteland sun and be longing for the dripping bushes I'd hidden in for the night. That's man for you. Want what you want 'til you get it and not a minute longer—one thing that held true for everyone. I needed it to.

I'm a scavenger. A prospector, merchant, trader. Thief, some might say. Living hand to mouth, fist to gut, knee to groin in a place where that made me the elite. Upper class because I wasn't starving on a rock farm, trying to convince myself weeds were corn. I wasn't collared up in a pen somewhere to be auctioned off or glassed out in a ditch, picking at scabs and wondering if it was the drugs or the rads making my skin want to leave my wasted body to seek its own fortune on the wind. Top of the mountain, that's me.

Thing is, mountaintops are small. Pointy. Easy to spit off the peak onto everyone below. Even easier to lose your footing and end up with them. And I don't care what they say, it's crowded at the top. Everyone clustered together, after the same stuff, trying to get it from each other without going over the edge. Glass, guns, and girls. Or guys. A market for everything.

That's how I stayed alive. I supplied the demand. Some of it, anyway. I was worth about a grand on the flesh market, but if I could bring some banger a 1200-cred payload, well, basic math is one of those few disciplines that survived the war.

Why don't they just take you, then, Jack? you ask, you clever devil. *When you bring them what they want, they can jump you, slap a collar on you. They can drop some glass down your throat or stick it right in your veins. Heck, put a gun to your head and tie you up, it doesn't matter.*

All valid points, my friend, and all reasons I talk fast and move faster. I usually know how long I can trust a contact, and I get out of the area before my time's up. If they catch me off guard, I have backup plans, and backups for those. That's how I stay alive. That's why, pulling my bag from the rocks where I'd hid it, I was careful not to jostle the Old World grenades tucked inside my pants. Survival.

My sister had taught me that, back when she was still around. *Survivors have contingencies,* she'd say. She'd said a lot of other stuff, too, like the day she broke the news that she wasn't really my sister. She'd found me when I was too young to remember and had been still mostly child herself. I had always assumed she was my sister until she pointed out that we couldn't be related, comparing her brown skin and curly black hair to my lighter tones. I had stubbornly asserted that that didn't mean we weren't family, and she had smiled and hugged me. *That's right,* she had said, and it wasn't until years later that I understood why there were tears in her eyes.

It was an hour's walk to Hammer's camp. Not too creative with their names, these bangers. I'd known two other Hammers, and both tried to kill me. Like I said, you could only trust these guys for so long before you had to get clear of them. Number three's time was up, but he didn't know it. I'd spent days on a bullet hunt for him, digging through corpses' pockets, busting open forgotten lockboxes, even collecting spent casings from places where firefights had left someone too rushed or too dead to gather them themselves. Even without powder or bullets, the brass had a little value, and Hammer had a guy in his crew who had the gear to reload them. They called him Loader.

I found the camp where I'd left it, more or less hidden in a gully in what passed for a wooded area a safe distance behind some old supermarket. A few skeletons of Old World furniture were scattered around, dragged there by previous users of the site. Three guys were sitting around a dilapidated table, playing cards and smoking. Loader was past them, working at his bench. Hammer was sprawled on a decaying couch, but he stood up and smiled when he saw me.

"Jackie boy," he said, spreading his arms in something that would have looked like a welcome from someone else. He wore a necklace of teeth he'd extracted with the claw hammer tucked into his belt. "Been three days. I thought you'd forgot us. Must have a damn big load if it took you that long. What do you got for me?"

Now here's the thing you need to understand about bangers. If they don't kill you on sight, most of them are pretty friendly. Loader had given me a wave when he saw me, and one of the card players nodded when our eyes met. But that friendliness will disappear real fast if you aren't careful, and you'll be lying in the dirt wondering where all your blood got to before you realize you said anything wrong. So I smiled back, mindful of all the guns and blunt objects in the vicinity.

"A little bit of this, a little bit of that," I said. I unslung the bag from my shoulder and started unloading it onto the card table as the bangers gathered around. One item at a time. Builds suspense.

First came a battered cigar box. "Thirty-eight special and three-fifty-seven," I said, flipping the box of bullets open. It wasn't a big box, but it was full. One of the men nodded, and I noticed he had a .38 on his hip.

Next came two dirty quart jars. One didn't have a lid, so I'd tied a scrap of some dead man's shirt with twine to cover the top. "Twenty-two LR. Found these in a collapsed basement. About 1200 rounds altogether."

After that were four magazines of .223, three boxes of 9mm, and a jar of various empty casings. Hammer stared at the ordnance on the table, arms crossed, not saying anything. I thought maybe the rads had finally got him, that the last of his brain had fried away right there in front of me, but then he finally spoke.

"Well, what do you want for it?"

I tell you, there's a reason "bright as a banger" isn't meant as a compliment.

"Seeing as I'm not packing at the moment, I wouldn't turn down a spare heater," I said. I gave my best casual, appraising nod at the firearms scattered about the camp. What I really wanted was some clean water and decent food, but I'd have better luck finding either of those under a rock somewhere than with Hammer's crew.

Hammer grunted at that, opened a rusted toolbox, and produced a battered revolver. I flipped the cylinder out and shook the gun, sprinkling the tabletop with sand and flecks of rust. At some point, a bug had clogged one of the chambers with a hardened nest of mud. I raised an eyebrow at Hammer. He was shorting me, bad.

"Looks more likely to kill me than anybody I point it at."

"What was you expecting, some Old World death ray? Better than nothing, ain't it?"

I shrugged. I couldn't push back too hard, but I had to try for a little more. "Slightly prettier than a rock, but not as aerodynamic. But maybe with some ammunition," I reached for one of the boxes on the table but was met with Hammer's polite refusal by way of a sawed-off shotgun prodding me in the ribs.

"You paid for a gun. Not bullets."

"Oh, that's right, I forgot." I fished in the cargo pockets of my pants for some spare bargaining chips and produced two handfuls of shotgun shells. "Twelve gauge. Just your size." I smiled.

Hammer faltered and then lowered the gun. Bangers *love* shotguns, and they've got to have something to shoot out of them. "One for one," he growled. We both knew he was ripping me off.

"Fair enough. Pleasure doing business with you." What can I say? I wasn't in the strongest bargaining position. I reached for the box of bullets again, but one of the other thugs grabbed my arm.

"Wait a minute. What else has he got in his pockets? He was trying to cheat us, boss."

"Hold on now, boys." I twisted my arm free but didn't reach for the bullets again. "Customers get the bag, but the pants are my private stock. My pockets have nothing to do with our agreement."

Hammer leveled his gun at me again. "Check his pockets."

I held up my hands and stepped away as the man who had grabbed me made to pat me down. "Whoa, now. I'm not so keen on the all the rubbing and grabbing. Tell you what, you can just have the pants. Sound fair?" I started untying the rope I used for a belt, inching closer to the table as I did.

Hammer and his boys weren't sure what to make of my sudden disrobing. That was the point. *Survivors have contingencies.* While the bangers were busy figuring out how to react, I pulled the pins on the grenades strapped just below my hip pockets.

The grenades hit the ground. The bangers stared. I jerked up my pants, grabbed a handful of bullets from the table, and ran, bullets in one hand and an empty gun in the other.

"Get down!" Hammer roared behind me, and the grenades roared back.

The first was a stun grenade, or so the stenciling on the side had said. As my ears rang and the concussion kicked me in the back, I was inclined to agree. The second grenade should have been spewing a cloud of tear gas at the bangers. I took the coughed obscenities and wildly off-target bullets chasing me through the sparse trees as a sign it had worked.

I didn't have much time to get away. The hornet nest had been kicked, and Hammer would be coming for me with a mind to do more than sting. So I did the only thing I could think to do, because even though my instincts were adamant that it was a bad idea, they couldn't come up with any better ones. I ran for the supermarket.

You learn things, living in the wastes. As a kid, I was lucky enough to have a sister that taught me a lot more than most people. But between teaching literacy, history, and science from memory and scavenged books, she also covered the basics, like where to run and how to hide once you got there. And right near the top of the list of places to avoid, just under military bases, were supermarkets.

They all got cleaned out when everything first went bad, she'd told me. *There's nothing left to find that you can't find easier somewhere else.* She was right. They were nothing but bait now—huge, empty promises of food and shelter ready to snap shut on anyone fool enough to believe them. Most were bases for whatever group of bangers were mean enough to take them from their previous owners. Of course, there's worse things than bangers in the world.

Hammer had chosen to make camp a respectable distance away. That boded well for my escape. As for staying alive after I got away from the wildly firing thugs behind me, I'd just have to hope Hammer's choice had been born of caution rather than any certainty of danger in the grocery store.

I cleared the trees, and there was nothing but a scramble up a rocky slope and a short sprint to the door between me and the back of the building. So up the slope I ran, at least, as well as a guy can run when the ground beneath him wants to play dodge-the-foot. The rocks were loose and eager to shift under my weight, but, after a stumble or two, I reached the top with my ankles intact. I wanted to stop, to catch my breath, but I was completely exposed. I kept running, and boy, did I regret it when the bullet hit.

My left hand jerked. Then it burned. Then I looked down and saw blood pouring from a place on the edge of my hand, where a fingertip-sized chunk of flesh had been a second before. I like to think I have a way with words, so it's embarrassing to admit that the string of unoriginal vocabulary I vomited up was a good approximation of the shouts that had chased me out of the woods.

I pressed the wound against my chest, trying to slow the bleeding as I stumbled over to a door. It wouldn't open, and I didn't dare try to force it. If someone was inside, the last thing

I wanted to do was announce my intrusion. I looked around for another entrance, and a bullet powdered the bricks above my head.

I ducked a little lower and ran along the wall to a loading dock. Two of the roll-up doors were shut, but the third was raised to knee high. I fell on my side and scooted under, trying not to aggravate the hole in my hand. My shoulder bumped the door as I rolled by, jarring loose whatever grip the years had placed on it, and it slammed into the concrete behind me like a guillotine. I held my breath as the metallic echoes of the impact chased themselves around the cinder block walls. A good thirty seconds later, I let myself breathe again as I got my bearings.

It was dim, but some light filtered through dirt-crusted windows. Outside, the gunfire had stopped. They must have figured I was as good as dead once I was inside. That, or they were on their way up the hill to find me and finish me off, but I like to stay optimistic.

I got to my feet, hand still pressed to my chest. My first order of business would have to be patching it up. There didn't seem to be any first aid kits around, nor much of anything else. The stockroom was all empty shelves and bare pallets. Anything edible had been carted off long ago. All that remained was a few scraps of faded, empty packaging and a corpse slouched against one wall.

A corpse. With clothes. I walked over and gave it a closer look. The body was a man's and had been there long enough to dry out but not entirely waste away. I took that as a good sign the store was uninhabited but still tried to keep quiet as I ripped off a strip from his shirt. It wasn't too dirty. I wrapped it tight around my wounded hand, finally setting down the few bullets I hadn't dropped when I got hit. There were four of them. I shrugged and loaded them into my rusty revolver. Could have been worse.

Gun loaded in case something jumped out at me and bleeding a little less than before, I patted down the body. Chances were he'd been stripped of anything worthwhile, but it never hurts to check. For all I knew, he'd hidden here just like me but had had the misfortune of catching his bullet somewhere more important than the hand. Nothing in his shirt, nothing in his pants, his shoes were too small for me. Then, paydirt. A bulge in his hip pocket. A flask! I unscrewed the cap and took a whiff. The fumes stabbed at my nostrils, and I could have cheered. I poured whatever alcoholic concoction it was over my makeshift bandage and sucked air through gritted teeth as it worked its antiseptic magic. The bandage had stopped the bleeding, and now I might even get to keep the hand.

"Thanks, pal," I whispered. I patted the dead man's shoulder. His leathery head creaked to one side.

I made my way to the swinging doors that separated the stockroom from the sales floor. I didn't see any signs of life through the scarred plastic windows, but I crouched low anyway as I slipped out.

There was a little more light out there, borne from the store's glass front on dusty bridges that fanned out and faded away as they strained to reach the back, where I crept along in front of an empty meat counter. It was quiet in that loud way big spaces have. Ancient salespapers cajoled into movement by stray drafts of air wheezed out dry breaths across the floor, and clumsily flying insects bounced off empty steel shelves like tiny echoes of the gunshots that had chased me there.

I made my way up one side—looted condiment shelves to my right, the deserted produce section to my left. The shriveled man in the stockroom was riper than anything left there. A glint caught my eye under the shelves, and I bent down to find an unopened jar of pickles. I smiled. Pickles never really go bad. I set my gun on a shelf to free my good hand and relished the pop of the jar's seal. That's not something you get to hear often out here, and the sour bite of decades-old, so-pickled-you-don't-really-have-to-chew-them pickles is an even rarer treat. Definitely better than scorpions.

Something clicked softly, out of sight. I swapped the pickle jar for my gun and dropped to a knee. From around the front endcap stepped an emaciated dog, nails tick-ticking on the tile floor. I stood up as tall as I could, gun leveled at the animal. Its lips curled back to show off teeth able to put the hole in my hand to shame. A low growl told me to leave, but it was too soon. Hammer could still be around.

"Don't do it, puppy," I said. I reached for the pickle jar, hoping it held enough of a peace offering to satisfy the starving animal. The dog charged.

POW-POW! POW!

The gun jerked in my hand, and the dog dropped with a whimper, one leg twitching feebly as it bled out on the supermarket floor. I sighed. Another victim of the wastes. So much for being quiet, but I couldn't risk it getting close.

Tick-tick-tick-tick.

I spun around just in time to sidestep the dead dog's snarling buddy, but it was already turning back on me. I grabbed the top shelf and jumped, hauling my feet up and out of the way just in time to keep the dog from clamping onto my ankle. I stretched forward, fingers scraping the bar that ran down the spine of the shelving unit. If I could get a grip, pull myself up on top—the shelves started to tilt.

"Swell."

I couldn't get clear. My back hit the floor, hard. An instant later, the shelves hit me, harder, a thundering tower of retail fixtures desperate to vent its displeasure with me. The top shelf caught me just below the ribs. The next two down got my thighs and shins. I gasped for air. I could barely move. Pickle juice soaked my shirt, I had dropped my gun, and I couldn't see the dog. With any luck, it had been crushed. I twisted and found the revolver lying just close enough to touch but too far to grab. Then I found the dog.

I can only explain its positioning as an inspired display of cunning because I had to have run out of bad luck to account for it. He was behind and to my left, creating a terribly awkward angle for shooting, pinned on my back as I was. That was assuming I could even reach the gun, which was stubbornly resisting my efforts to do more than graze it with my fingertips.

The dog crept closer. It barked, the raspy sound of starvation harsh and loud in the deserted supermarket. It was wary after the collapse of the shelves, and that caution gave me an opportunity. I sucked in a breath, strained for an extra inch of reach, and grabbed the gun. The dog barked its displeasure at my movements. I twisted and stretched and tried to draw a bead on it. The dog took another step.

POW!

My last bullet clipped the dog's ear and buried itself in a faded picture of a tomato on the far wall. The dog yelped in pain, then ran at me. I held the gun like a club. If my timing was good and my luck better, I might be able to kill it. Crack its skull, maybe choke it, or snap its neck. If not, well, I'd rather fill a fellow survivor's stomach than some banger's necklace of trophy teeth.

The dog reached me. I swung the revolver and smacked it across the snout. It snapped at my neck and caught the left hand I reflexively brought up in defense. A long canine tooth sank into my bullet wound, and I screamed. I flailed at the beast's head with an empty gun it refused to acknowledge in its determination to amputate my hand.

Fzap.

A flash of red light, and the dog crumpled. I pulled my mauled hand out of its mouth. Lots of blood. I was panting, my head twisting back and forth in a panic I hadn't felt for a while. What had happened? That light—then I saw him.

At the end of the aisle was a boy, maybe nine years old, silhouetted against the light leaking through the front windows. He came closer, narrowed eyes never leaving me. He held an Old World laser pistol corded to a power supply belt. The pain and disbelief reached the tipping point in my brain, and I had to laugh, even if it came out as a weak cough. Here I was, covered in pickle juice, hand a mangled mess, losing more blood by the second, and my life was in the hands of a kid with better hardware than the professional killers I'd run here to escape.

Standing over me, the kid prodded my head with his toe. "Who are you?"

"Name's Jack." It came out softer than I'd meant. My voice was going or my hearing was. "You—you look like my sister."

I passed out. Ω

*Read the next exciting chapter of **Deal Gone Bad** in Issue 2 of*
Nonlocal Science Fiction!

Nonlocal Science Fiction

nonlocalscifi.com

Thanks for reading Issue #1!

We'll be back with our second issue in June 2015!

Be sure to follow us on social media so you never miss a thing!

facebook.com
/NonlocalScifi

twitter.com
/NonlocalSciFi